W9-AEV-206

Wolfskin

Weekly Reader Children's Book Club *presents*

WOLFSKIN

by Lillian Pohlmann

W · W · NORTON & COMPANY · INC ·
New York

Library of Congress Catalog Card No. 68-16570

Published simultaneouly in Canada by
George J. McLeod Limited, Toronto
Printed in the United States of America
Weekly Reader Children's Book Club Edition
Senior Division

For my grandson,
David Mac Innes

Contents

Wolfskin

Cheechako Johnny

1

IT WAS A MURKY April day in 1898 and Johnny Clemens, tall and lean for his twelve years, stood dejectedly at the ship's rail. Gray eyes brooding, straw-colored hair blowing in the wind, he couldn't wait to leave the filthy overcrowded ship; yet all that he had seen of Alaska made him shiver with dread. Crowding down to the water were the closed dark forests or the great gloomy mountains, sealed with glaciers. On board ship it was all noise. Out there, except for the occasional boom of cracking ice, there was silence.

Johnny looked down into the slate-colored churning water of Lynn Canal, the narrow inland sea they'd been steaming through all day, and watched the endless side roll of water from the prow. When he looked up, his father was beside him, pointing at something that looked like a small pier far ahead.

"That's the place, all right," an old sailor told them. "Become an ugly little bully of a town, it has, too. Takes all comers and tries to outsmart 'em all. It swaggers, that's what it does — cocky, as though it didn't have those brutes of mountains baying at its back."

"What d'you mean?" his father asked. "There must be some law. It's United States territory. Has been for thirty years."

"*Seward's Folly. Seward's Icebox. Seward's Polar-Bear Garden.* Anything they used to call it still goes. And more besides." The old man laughed. "You'll see."

"We will indeed." His father's eyes were shining. "You stay right here, son. Save my place. I'll get the boys."

Johnny tried. But as the pier drew closer and its small human figures grew nearer to life size, it was impossible to hold his own on deck. It swarmed with shoving, cursing, laughing men, shouldering their packs or wrestling with bundles and boxes. Before he could find his father or either of his father's partners, Pete Keyes or Sam Gill, ropes were being thrown out and a few men, too excited to wait, had splashed over the side to wade ashore.

"Pa! Here! *Here*!" The din was terrific. Johnny tried to pull away until his father could reach him; but, pushed forward by a tide of impatient miners, he was on the gangplank before he knew it. Startled at its narrow wobbliness, he took a great breath and walked carefully down to shore.

Johnny's father, and Pete, and Sam came soon after. They paced restlessly, waiting for their outfits to be dumped on the beach, then piled them quickly to one side and walked together toward town.

The narrow streets, lined with a hodgepodge of buildings were crowded with men. Signs, blatant over doorways, announced miners' outfitting stores, saloons, a bakery, boarding houses, dance halls, a tinsmith shop, drugs, and groceries. The sound of a piano and rowdy singing came through one doorway, the smell of fresh bread from another. Across the street a crowd of gold seekers argued excitedly together.

"I'm going to see what's going on," Pete said. "See you later."

Sam went with him, and Johnny and his father moved on. A fierce wind watered their eyes and snapped the American flag flying from a pole over their heads. Johnny frowned as mud splashed over his shoes and legs from a horse and buggy rattling by.

His father burst out laughing. "Cheer up, Johnny," he said. "We made it!"

Johnny grinned at him. "I thought this was just the beginning."

"Fair enough. Anyway, so far so good." He stopped to read a sign. "Bee Kay Trading Post. Shall we try it?"

They climbed the steps and were crossing the wide porch to the doorway when a big wolflike dog roared straight at them.

Johnny jumped back. "Get out of here!" he yelled.

"All right, fellow. It's all right." His father spoke quietly to the dog as it sniffed and growled at Johnny's heels. "So you're a husky, eh? And a beauty, too. Johnny," he said low, "it's your acting so fearful makes a dog rush you. I told you that time and time again."

"I can't help it."

"Sure you can. Just because Big Shep mauled you when you were knee high, doesn't mean every dog will. Besides you're a big kid now."

Johnny didn't feel very big. He gave the dog a wide berth, and walked nervously into the store.

A girl was standing there. "Hello, *Cheechako*," she said.

Cheechako? Johnny didn't know what she meant, so he ignored her as he did his little cousins when they got fresh. He moved away, examining the shelves of groceries and miners' supplies: lanterns, frying pans, tin cups, picks, and shovels, tables of men's shirts and pants and boots, bolts of cloth, a barrel of beans and another of dried fish, a table of animal skins. One fur was so beautiful Johnny had to touch it. By letting the silver tips of the hairs brush his palm, he felt a scary aliveness in it. That dog out there would probably feel like this, he thought.

Slowly, back and forth, his hand moved over the fur as he listened to the storekeeper and his father. "You'd do better to take rice than beans," the storekeeper said. "Nourishing and much lighter to carry. Goes fine with game too, should you shoot any."

"Wild game, yes." From the way his father said it, Johnny could tell he was hatching another dream. A tiny one this time, of steaming rice and roast bird, served up in style beside their campfire. It was fun to play along with the small dreams, but the big ones. . . . He sighed, remembering all his father's gold and silver dreams, all the promises of sudden wealth.

Johnny had been born near one of those dreams, a silver mine in Nevada. After his mother's death, when he was five, he'd gone from one mining camp to another, being boarded with various families while his father prospected or, if pressed for ready money, worked for others for a day's pay.

Instead of the steady places and faces most kids knew, Johnny's memory was a jumble of both – the places stretched from dusty settlements and camps in the Nevada desert through at least a dozen gold towns of the California Mother Lode, to San Francisco. And so many faces, most of them as dim to him now as old photographs, hung helter-skelter in a smoky room.

Aunt May used to nag Johnny's father every time she saw him. "You're not being fair to Johnny," she'd say. "Just because your way of life satisfies you, you think it will him. But John, it hasn't. He's too quiet – timid, too – for a boy. What he needs is proper family life and schooling. Let him come with us."

Johnny had squirmed at her calling him timid, as if she knew how he felt when he was alone too much. Otherwise, he'd tried not to care either way. She'd been talking a long time and hadn't changed anything.

Yet one day his father had seemed to hear her. He looked at Johnny longer and harder than usual, rubbed his hand across his eyes, and said he knew she was right. Johnny had liked living in San Francisco with Aunt May, Uncle Bill, and his little cousins, Lucy and Jim. Though he missed his father terribly and worried at first about fitting into city life, he thought he was going to be all right. After a few months, he was feeling almost easy there, almost happy.

It was after he started school and became friendly with some of the boys that his father came to see Johnny about the newest dream.

"Johnny, they've struck gold in Canada, near Dawson City in the Klondike. A couple of fellows want me to go. They say we can go in a hurry by way of Alaska. Take a ship there, pack over the mountains by way of the Yukon, and we're on our way to riches, for once. Let's go!"

"Oh John!" Aunt May said. "Not again!"

His father had merely smiled until later when he and Johnny were alone. "It isn't only that I believe we should share this great venture, Johnny. It's that you're being too coddled here. Aunt May, bless her, watches over you as though you were as young as her own. Babies her husband, too, for that matter. Anyway, this chance is too big for you and me not to take it together."

"Pa, listen. I like it here."

His father had hugged him as though he'd heard, but his eyes had been unseeing, too full of dream, the way they were now.

"Rice? What do you think, Johnny? Shall we take on another ten pounds? Is it true," he asked the storekeeper, "that the Canadian border patrol sends you back if you aren't carrying enough food to keep you for a while? We outfitted ourselves rather thoroughly in San Francisco, we thought, but. . . ."

It was hard for Johnny to listen because of the way the girl stood there, smiling and looking him up and down.

"Well?" he asked her, finally.

"You don't know what *cheechako* means, do you?"

He shrugged.

"It only means that you're new to Alaska. It's the opposite of being a *sourdough*. You can't be a sourdough till you've stayed here for at least a year. I'm a real one because I was born here. Where'd you get so many freckles?" She laughed.

"California. Where'd you think?"

"Kiska – he's the dog that scared you – acts wild but he isn't. Not really."

Johnny frowned and pretended to look over her head.

"Don't talk the boy to death, Elie," the storekeeper told her, and he turned back to Johnny's father. "It excites her to see a newcomer anywhere near her own age. Very few gold seekers bring their children with them as you probably know, Mr. . . ."

"Clemens. Senior and junior. John and Johnny."

"I'm Kirov. Boris Kirov. You're fresh off the boat, I take it."

"Yes. And due to a double-crossing captain, embarrassingly short of cash. Paid the devil full fare in cash before we left Frisco, but when he saw the mob of would-be Klondikers on the pier in Seattle, his memory failed. Told us we'd paid to Seattle only and would have to pay again or get off."

Mr. Kirov shook his head. "There's too much of that kind of business going on."

"So, we're not able to spend much. But how's your stock of advice? Do you agree with us that the Chilkoot Pass is the best and fastest way to get through the mountains into Canada?"

"Chilkoot or White Pass, both are killers. Take one and you'll wish you took the other."

"Mr. Kirov's trying to frighten us, Johnny."

"No, I wouldn't do that. It's just that I've been here all my life. My Russian ancestors settled here in 1810. When the United States bought Alaska Territory, they got me with it. Mrs. Kirov is American. Her folks came here from the states as missionaries and started a school."

But John Clemens wasn't listening. "How do you get to the Chilkoot from here?" he asked impatiently.

"Only one trail goes out of town to the gorge. It's well marked by now, believe me. Follows the river part way. When you get to the place called Sheep Camp, you'll wish you were part goat. That's what's needed then, the stamina and skill of a mountain goat. You're not figuring on going it alone are you? You and the boy?"

"No. Got a couple of partners."

Johnny's father laughed and Mr. Kirov went on, "If you'll excuse my saying so, Mr. Clemens, you're all a pack of darned fools. I've seen gold strikes before. Alaska, Canada, it's always the same. For every one who gets his gold, a thousand break their backs and hearts."

"I'm a mining man, Kirov. Been to. . . ."

"April or not, it snowed heavy in those mountains last week. You might have to wait a while. What's more, there's thirty thousand fortune hunters in the Klondike country already. Swarming, they are."

"You could leave your son here," the girl interrupted. "He could go to school with me and help Papa in the store."

"That he could." Kirov laughed. "Mrs. Kirov helps some but I'd rather she wouldn't. Elie either. I like my women to be women. Besides," he added, mussing his daughter's hair, "with this new breed that's coming in here. . . . I tell you a businessman needs all his wits and a hundred eyes. I took on a young fellow to work for me last month. Nice fellow, he was, and just learning to be of some help when he got the gold fever and off he went. How about it?" he asked Johnny.

Johnny grinned at his joking. "I think I'll stick with my father."

"It's going to be a hard haul." His father was looking at him, perfectly serious. "I see that now."

"But Pa, we've seen it all the time!"

"Yes, we have, haven't we? It was going to toughen us up, wasn't it?" He winked at Kirov. "Very well, let's get on with it." He paid for the rice and looked around. "Anything else we need, Johnny? You think you'll be warm enough?"

"I think he'd like that fur," the girl said.

Johnny jerked his hand away from it. "Why should I?"

"You want that?" John Clemens picked it up and turned it over, looking at the cleanness of its underside. "You want it for wrapping around you inside your bedroll? Or, inside your coat, if need be?"

"That'd be silly," Johnny said.

"On the contrary," Kirov told him. "It would be very sensible. Ever hear of a wolf freezing to death?"

The girl giggled.

"I'll be warm enough, Pa. Come on." Johnny flushed with embarrassment.

"A fur could be quite a comfort to a boy," his father said.

Kirov agreed. "A comfort now. And later, when he's grown, he can spread it before a fire and be at home anywhere."

"But if we're already short of money. . . ." Johnny began.

"We'll hire one less packer. Good backs we have,

Johnny. Warm fur we have not. How much, Kirov?"

"Thirty-five dollars."

"Papa!" the girl squealed. "Why so much? When you gave the Indian only six pounds of tea for it?"

"Upstairs!" her father roared. She hesitated, not looking at all troubled. "Upstairs! Now!" Kirov rolled the fur and slipped it under Johnny's arm. "Take it for twenty," he said, "I'd like to see the boy have it."

"Let him pay you after he finds gold, Papa," Elie called from the top of the stairs and her father smiled.

"You heard the little lady," he said to them. "Now take it along."

John Clemens shook his head and opened his purse. Johnny could tell by its thinness that there wasn't much in it. So could Mr. Kirov. "Ten dollars is all I'll take. That's what the tea cost me," he said, and laughing, he shook his fist at the girl.

Johnny's father laughed too. "Fifteen then. A fellow in business ought to make an honest profit," he said, as they shook hands. "Good-by and thanks."

"Getting started in the morning?"

"That's right."

"Good luck, then."

Johnny folded the fur, put it inside his coat, and looked up. The girl was still standing at the top of the stairs.

She waved. "Good-by, *Cheechako* Johnny."

On the Trail

2

THAT EVENING Johnny caught some of the crazy gold fever that was burning in the miners all around him. Though the wind froze the breath in his throat, he felt warm and excited inside, the scared part of himself gone, for a change. He felt especially so after his father, who had been too quiet after leaving the trading post, began to act light-hearted again.

Another boat had arrived after theirs, and rooms and boarding houses were filled to overflowing. Tents, including Johnny's and his father's small one, bloomed on vacant lots, between buildings, and along the shore, like mushrooms. The doors of restaurants, saloons, and dance halls swung in and out to jangling music, shouting, and laughter.

On the street, men bargained with Indian packers or sorted their gear, adding newly bought items. Others, wanting to lighten their loads, tried to sell articles that now appeared useless to them. An old man hammered away at a makeshift wagon.

Because word had got round that a frozen trail was easier to walk than a slushy one, the bitter cold hung like a promise. When clouds parted to show one pale star, Johnny and his father joined in the wild cheers.

Back in their tent, they were sober again. "It's going to be a cold one," his father said of the night. "Better spread out that wolfskin."

Johnny reached gingerly for it in the dark, tossed it over his blankets, and quickly folded himself under them to get warm.

John Clemens spread his bedding between Johnny and the tent flap, took off his boots, crawled in, and said good night. In the morning, his boots were gone.

Furious, Johnny's father borrowed some shoes from Pete and stalked back to the Bee Kay Trading Post. Johnny went with him, bracing himself for a meeting with the dog, but Kiska wasn't there.

The girl was. Brown hair braided over her head, blue eyes shining, she was all smiles until John Clemens announced the reason they'd come. Then she looked like the end of the world. "Oh Papa, did you hear that?"

"Your boots, you say. Blackguards!" Kirov shook his head. "With all due respect to you, Mr. Clemens, you and other honorable men, a gold strike attracts the scum of the earth. In the old days . . . but you don't want to hear about the old days. Sit down, here. What size?"

"Elevens."

"I'd advise mukluks. Indian boots. Caribou skin is a lot better on the trail than hobnails. Cheaper too."

Johnny leaned against the counter and looked down at his own hobnailed boots.

"I wish you would," Elie said.

"Would what?"

"Stay here."

While John Clemens tried on boots, Elie talked to Johnny about Alaska — the animals that lived there, how nights would be light soon, the flowers, the warm summers.

She's bragging about things as though she's trying to sell them, Johnny thought.

"Nobody near my age *ever* stays," she added.

Why should they stay in this dump of a place? he felt like asking her. Except for a few decent houses, there was nothing but shacks, tents, gambling places, and mud. It was only a jumping-off place to the gold country, where a man couldn't even go to sleep without having his boots stolen.

Any excitement Johnny had felt last night was gone. Even the promise of fair weather had been broken. The air, as he and his father walked back to their tent, was gray and cold with a drizzle that blotted out the mountains.

"Do we start now?" he asked.

His father sighed deeply. "We'd better think it over."

"What d'you mean?"

"Perhaps you should go back to Aunt May and the family, on the boat tomorrow."

"Pa!" His own voice startled him, coming so shrill. "What's the matter? You think I'm too young? That I'll hold you back or something?"

His father gave a short laugh. "I've been realizing I might have overpersuaded you, that, in fact, I gave you no choice but to come. So, I'm giving you a choice now."

"No. I want to be with you."

"Couple of days out of Frisco, I started thinking about it. Whether I shouldn't send you back."

"Wouldn't that cost money?"

"Yes." He sighed again. "I guess it would. But the way you've been acting. . . ."

"Pa, listen! I'm here now. If you go, I go."

"That's the way you feel?" His father looked hard at him. "Honest?"

"Sure."

"All right then, let's get to our packs. The boys have the stuff lined up and are ready to go."

With so many men hanging around town, Johnny thought there might not be many on the trail. But there was a steady stream of miners, many pulling sleds or squeaky wagons loaded with their gear. A few had horses or dog teams, and others had hired Indian packers to share the bulk of their burdens. Some sang together as they plodded along, some cursed or shouted, and some were silent. Fog had cut them off from the frightening bigness of Alaska, but Johnny could still sense it — it and those brutes of mountains waiting to test them.

Sometimes the trail climbed up and was strewn with boulders. Sometimes it went down through melting snow and icy water with forests close on either side. It was an endless day, and when they finally stopped Johnny was glad they set up camp close to the others. Their laughing and teasing and calling out to each other sounded cozy to him. It was almost as though they were a family.

Later, as they sat around the huge comforting campfire, talk drifted from tales of gold finds to accounts of encounters with all kinds of wild animals: grizzlies, wolves, elk, and an angry bull moose. Johnny, nervous and fascinated at the same time, moved closer to his father. Several times he turned to examine the dusk behind him, the near upthrust slope, the twisted trees. By bedtime, with the glow from the fire showing through the flimsy sides of the tent, he longed for firm, protective walls and a safer bed.

"Johnny, here." His father stood with the wolfskin in his hands. "Let me show you how to keep warm with this thing."

"Golly, Pa!" he spoke crossly so that his father couldn't see how much the men's talk had frightened him. "I'm a little old for the baby bunting stuff, you know."

"I'm not." John Clemens draped the wolfskin over Johnny's shoulders and fastened it around him by knotting the skins of the legs. "Your father's hunting bound, all right. For gold, to buy a bigger skin to wrap his long-legged Johnny in." Chanting the old nursery rhyme in his own way, he grabbed Johnny, wolfskin and all, in a great hug. They stood so for a long, hushed moment, and it seemed to Johnny that his father, also, was trembling.

The next day they had to cross the river on a crude log ferry. It dipped perilously, water sloshing over their boots as they got on. Pushing off, it dipped again, and Johnny had to keep himself from leaping back onto land.

He was afraid to watch and afraid not to as the river, bigger and wilder, now they were on it, seemed determined to fling them about. Midway, caught in a great swirling flow, the raft swung all the way around and threatened to capsize before the ferryman got it under control.

A half hour later they were back on the trail, picking their way along the soggy edge of a marsh. Suddenly, ahead of Johnny, a heavily loaded horse shied sideways away from a barking dog and into the bog. Almost immediately he was in too deep to get out and had to be shot.

Johnny's father, who had been turning at regular intervals to ask Johnny, "How're you doing?" exchanged looks with his partners and said nothing.

Johnny swallowed hard and moved on. There was no more use in shouting out in anger over the death of a horse than in complaining over the weight on his back or the burning of pack straps against his shoulders. If only he'd been able to save the horse, somehow, and have it for his own. He wondered what that would be like and how his cousins might act if he arrived home astride it.

He thought of things he'd write to Aunt May and Uncle Bill that they would never believe. He thought of the hope that kept the men on the trail going, *going*. He pictured a big bubble of hope over each gold seeker's head, pretending a little gold in some and more in others. For a few of the hopers he imagined gold standing in tall stacks of coins, like those he'd glimpsed in a gambling hall. For none did he have the heart to imagine no gold at all.

The hours ran into each other. Time seemed no time finally, only steps. Lifting feet and putting them down in and out of muck and snow. Over snow-splotched rocky plateaus that climbed like mountains leading to mountains, day was an endless stumbling, back-loaded pain. Night was no load with the pain still there in aches and bruises and blisters.

On the night before the big climb, the mist lifted and the glow of snowy mountain heights moved nearer. Johnny, huddling by the fire and chewing on tinned beef folded into a flapjack, saw it. So did the others. They grinned at each other.

"Now the adventure *really* begins," said his father.

"The big haul, you mean," said Sam.

"How many trips do you think it'll take to get the stuff up?"

"Maybe one'll do it."

They watched quietly for a while until a sudden roar, like thunder, vibrated above them.

"What's that?"

A big burly man who had just come back down the

pass answered. "It's nothin'. Just nothin' but a big old glacier crackin' away up there some place."

Johnny had been surprised to learn that not all in camp were on their way in. Some were returning. Three men had appeared an hour earlier, loaded with gear that had been shed by climbing miners. They said they made a business of getting such stuff back to town where they would sell it to newcomers all over again.

Johnny was finishing up with tea, the cup good and hot between his hands, when two more men appeared from the direction of the pass. Their faces, as they came slowly into the campfire light, looked stunned and one man kept shaking his head. They took the steaming mugs offered them with trembling hands; and it wasn't until they'd looked around and sipped a while that they began, slowly, to speak.

"There was three of us started out and. . . . It was around noon, or was it after that?"

"After," the other man said.

"Mac – MacNab his name was – went off the trail. Said he was going an easier way. Hadn't gone five steps, no time for a squeak even, before snow started sliding and he was gone like he was never there. Buried with it at the bottom of an abyss."

At first, frightened and dreadfully shaken, they spoke only of facts. But as Johnny, his father and the others gathered closer to listen, their voices rose with bitterness as they blamed Alaska, the late spring, the mountains, wind, and fate. Pointing then, they blamed an Indian boy standing by.

"There's the one. Been watching him and he's the one, all right. It's his fault. Supposed to go with us, help us, show us the way. He promised, then backed out."

"Not true." The Indian boy stepped forward, eyes flashing. "I tell you not to go. I say, mountain not ready. I say to you, 'wait,' but I cannot make you do it."

When neither man looked at him or answered him, he walked away.

Johnny ran after him. "Indian, listen! Will the mountain be ready tomorrow?" he asked.

"My name is Luke."

"Well, will it, do you think?"

The roar of a waterfall came to Johnny's ears with the far groaning of the glacier. When the Indian boy raised his eyes to the sky, Johnny lifted his also. Though shabby and dull as old Christmas ornaments, a few stars *were* there.

"Would you say they're a pretty good sign?" asked Johnny.

For the first time the Indian boy smiled. "I think all right you go in the morning."

Killer Pass

3

JOHNNY WOKE from a nightmare of falling snow with a knot of fear in his stomach. His body felt hot in the wolf-skin and his feet were icy cold. Already he could hear sounds of bustling, calling, and loading. It was morning.

"Pa?"

His father sat up fast. "Are the boys out? Do we go?" He groaned as he pushed his heavily socked feet into his mukluks. "These things are as stiff as I am."

"Flapjacks and coffee are on." Sam's voice came from outside. "You comin', John?"

Outside the tent, Johnny shivered under a gray, windy sky. "It doesn't look like a very good day to me."

"Maybe not, kid." Pete tossed coffee grounds at the fire. "But plenty of guys seem to think so."

He was right. The camp was emptying fast.

Johnny and his father gulped down some breakfast and joined the others just as a watery sun broke from the clouds.

Such a short distance, they'd heard, but *what* a distance. Shading his eyes to try to see the pass ahead Johnny saw only a snowy wall with small dark figures, moving slowly up it. How could they ever climb *that*? How, topheavy with packs, could they keep themselves from falling backward?

Falling backward was Johnny's big fear at first. Later, as sunshine and the steady digging in of many boots melted the trail to a slippery mud, he was afraid of side-stepping off it into nowhere as others had done. Later still, he feared he couldn't make it at all.

At every move the pack straps cut more deeply into his flesh; his back felt as though it were broken; his feet were numb. His breath scraped in his throat; his hands were cut and bleeding from clawing at rock and he was sick of trying to act like a man when he wasn't. Then all his fears became as nothing in the face of a new one.

He had been moving automatically, passing some men,

being passed by others, following his father. He had been thinking how those with horses were the luckiest, forgetting himself just long enough to feel sorry for a dog sprawled under its burden. At least humans knew where they were going and why. Pa does, anyway, he thought, and was relieved to see his father stop and sink down. It was about time they rested again.

When Johnny caught up to him, his father had an odd look on his face, a surprised look, and he was gasping.

Johnny crouched quickly beside him. "Pa! You all right?"

His father nodded without looking up. After a moment, he dragged himself out of the way of the climbers and lay down on his right side.

"I'll loosen the straps on your pack."

"Wait." The words came so faintly, Johnny could scarcely hear them. "Wait. Rest a little. You, too."

Johnny sat there, the new fear in his heart growing. The day, quite sunny now, spread out before them almost too pretty to bear. The great peaks were splotched with purple shade and blazing snow, the white slopes, dark-notched with the green of pointed trees. Near Johnny's hand, in a pocket of rock, a yellow flower was beginning to open.

Most climbers were too laden down and weary to think of helping anyone but themselves. Still, a few called out encouragement as they passed. "Take her easy, pard." "Could use a little rest like that, myself." "Poor devils." "Aren't we all?"

When one man and then another asked if they could do something to help, Johnny's father waved them on.

"Johnny?" He turned slowly and sat up.

"Yes?"

"Ready to go?"

"If you are."

"Yes . . . well . . . I guess we've been taking it a little too fast. What's the big hurry, huh? We'll slow down. 'T isn't as though we have to keep up with the boys. We'll see 'em on top."

"Sure."

"And once we're there, no hurry at all. We'll camp by the lake. Many lakes, they say. We'll take our time. Make a small boat for crossing. Camp before we get to a lake if we want to."

"You sick, Pa?"

"A passing thing. From altitude, likely." He straightened, groaned, and covered his face with his hands. "I suppose I should lighten my load," he said at last.

"I'll take it."

A little smile flicked across his father's face. "You traveling too light?"

"We can change loads. Please, Pa."

"I'll be fine." He heaved to his feet, his face gray.

They dragged on slowly, so slowly that the summit seemed to move with them instead of coming closer. Johnny's eyes burned and his face and lips felt blistered and swollen, but none of that mattered now. If only his father. . . . He was afraid to move his eyes from the bent form ahead of him. If only Pete or Sam, missing them, would come back. Pa would *have* to let them help.

When his father faltered again, Johnny was beside him at once. As he helped him to lie down beside the trail, he saw someone coming down the slope, walking fast and easy and sure. It was the Indian boy returning after packing for some others over the top.

Johnny waved and called out, and in a moment Luke was on one knee beside him and his father. With Johnny's help, he quickly unfastened the pack and swung it to his own back. "Not far now," he said.

John Clemens nodded, his face twisted and changed as he forced himself carefully to his feet.

Johnny grabbed his hand. "Pa, please. Please don't try to go on if you can't, if you shouldn't. Please."

His father said nothing but kept hold of Johnny's hand and with Luke helping on his other side, they reached the top. There, in a confusion of piled outfits, tents, men, animals, and campfires, John Clemens let himself sink down. "The boys will find us here," he gasped.

With fear like a cry stuck in his throat, Johnny stretched

out his bedroll beside his father, helped him onto it, and gave him water to drink. Luke made a fire, and together they set up the tent over the sick man.

Sam found them there. He and Pete had pitched camp "a little up the line" hours before. "Pete's all in, so I came back to look for you. We didn't know you were having trouble, John," he said, his big face drooping.

"No trouble a little rest won't put to rights." John Clemens's voice, though low, was almost jaunty.

Johnny almost believed him. Sam did. "But," Sam said, and he pointed out to Johnny where he could be found, "should you need us, send the Indian."

All night the Indian kept the fire going, and Johnny stayed close to his father, offering him food and watching over him. John Clemens sipped the strong black coffee held to his lips but would not eat. For a while he seemed to sleep. Then he opened his eyes and reached for Johnny. "We made it, son," he whispered.

Before full light came again, he was dead. Sam and Pete helped Luke bury him while Johnny walked numbly through it all as if it were a nightmare.

Later, he couldn't remember whether it had been a gray or sunny day. He remembered only that the wind blew. He remembered nodding yes, he would go back home. Yes, that Sam and Pete could have his father's share of food supplies. Yes, they could pay him later when they returned rich to San Francisco. No, he couldn't think of anything they could do for him.

Johnny remembered that after an awful blankness of time, he had groped his way into the tent, crawled under the blankets, and let his wild sobs come. He slept, finally, woke up sobbing, slept and woke and tried to sleep again. If only he could stop the ache of his sadness. If only he weren't so alone and afraid. He cursed the gold rush and the men who'd first told his father about it, cursed Alaska for killing him. Why hadn't his father said that the climb was straining his heart? Why hadn't he, Johnny, turned back after seeing that first stricken look on his father's face. "Why?" he screamed. "Why? Why?"

He lay very still and when there was no answer, no sound but the wind, he sat up. "Luke!" he shrieked.

Almost at once, the broad bronzed face was looking in at him. "I'm here."

"I thought you'd gone. You know, packing for someone else who'd got the money to pay. Why didn't you?"

Luke walked away, his eyes as untelling as a secret and Johnny thought, what's to keep him from taking the money Pa had? He put a hand over his pocket where it was — the old purse with its twenty-dollar gold piece, two fives, and some change, before he remembered that it was Luke who had found it in his father's coat and had given it to him.

When Luke returned with a chunk of dried fish for him, Johnny turned from it, pulled on his boots and went out. Bypassing Luke's fire in a lee of rock, he stumbled, half-running, into the wind. If only he could be back into last year, last week, any time before yesterday or now.

Furiously he stopped, grabbed a rock and hurled it into the dusk. He hurled another and another and another as darkness blew over him, gripping each stone as though to bruise it, hurling each one as though to destroy it and stopped only when he was too exhausted to throw another.

Aware suddenly of the vastness of the night, he crouched, whimpering, close to the earth. It would be dark in the house in San Francisco, too, but warm and cozy as night should be. He thought of the family peacefully sleeping, never imagining what had happened here. If only he and his father could be back with them. San Francisco might be thousands of miles away but he'd get back there. He had to. It was all that mattered now, getting back down that killer cliff and out to where he could get a boat, fast, for home. He wished it were morning so he could start.

Half frozen, though he wore most of the clothes he had with him, he crept back to the fire. He hugged himself beside it without speaking, his head resting on his knees. He was almost asleep when Luke shook him.

Johnny looked up to see rivers of colored light flowing all across the sky. Purples and greens and yellows and blues moved slowly, as though to some great music.

"What is it?" he whispered at last.

"Northern lights."

"Has it happened before?"

"In our sky, many times."

The blues blurred to rosiness, like a banner arched across the sky. Then all brightness darkened into night. The wind roared, noisily again, and the great stars shone, close and blue-cold.

Johnny watched the firelight move over Luke's face and wished fiercely that the Indian were someone else, someone more like himself. There isn't anyone, he thought, no one *anywhere* that I can talk to. He felt angry again, as though the skies had let him hope for something that couldn't happen.

In the tent, he threw himself face down on his bedroll and lay still, trying to keep his mind empty. He thought of the wolfskin, and sprang up, fumbling frantically through the blankets until he found it. He shuddered as he carefully fitted and fastened it around him as his father had done. Then he curled himself up and went to sleep.

Luke's Home

4

Johnny was awakened by Luke breaking up wood for the fire, and he knew it was morning. For the first time since his father's death he felt the stiff soreness of his own body. Everything that was him, he thought, every part of his spirit and body, hurt. He started to moan, to pull the blankets over his head, then he kicked them back with sudden impatience. He had to get home.

He got up, unfastened the wolfskin, rolled it carefully into his bedding, and went out.

Luke poured him a cup of steaming tea. "All right we go soon?"

Johnny nodded and dug into a sack for some dried beef. "You want some of this?"

They ate quickly, washing the beef down with the tea. They took the tent down, but when Luke started to make a pack of it and the other things of his father's, Johnny protested. "I don't want them unless you do. They're no good to me. I'm going back to San Francisco."

"You will need money. Trading post will buy."

"If you want to bother," Johnny was anxious to leave. "And don't worry, I'll split with you."

Luke turned to him. "I do not worry." His eyes flashed as he tightened the straps on the pack and swung it over his back. "I do what I do and I ask for no thing."

He set out, walking so fast Johnny was afraid he couldn't keep up. Following behind, he splashed through the thin ice of snow-water puddles and kicked at the ice particles rimming the mud. He felt exhausted almost before they'd got started.

Sunrays ricocheted from the mountains and the snow. Distances were blinding, and the long endless way down became an unbearable reminder of the agonizing way up.

Steady lines of men were climbing as they had been before, toiling, cursing, slipping, resting with their gear, or puffing after their Indian packers. Several wondered aloud why a boy would be returning alone with an Indian, but Johnny ignored them.

When Luke suggested rest, Johnny would stop, but only for a few minutes. Limping now, his eyes burning and watering, he struggled on toward the one thing he wanted: to be back with Aunt May and Uncle Bill – his kind of people, who would understand his feelings – to be with the cousins, who, glad to see him, would be likely to climb all over him and keep him from thinking for a while. Back, boat, home. Doggedly he kept going to that beat, back, boat, home.

That evening Luke proposed that they return by way of his village. "My people live by inland sea. Tlingit Indians, Chilkat Tribe. Hunt and fish since old time," he said, adding, "my mama will make a healing for your eyes."

"No thanks. I have to hurry."

"Village is near, nearer than town if we follow river. Better for you."

He spoke gently and, for a moment, seemed to Johnny like any other boy. "Do you have your own language?" he asked Luke.

"We have." There was pride in his voice and Johnny thought how his father would have admired that. His father, always interested in new and different people and things, would have liked to visit an Indian village. Tears burned like acid in Johnny's eyes as Luke continued.

"We have also words from Russians who came in big ships and stay long. And United States words from missionaries who make schools where I go for a while. You will come?"

Johnny buried his head in his arms. More than anything he wanted to say no, but what if Luke should then go anyway and leave him alone. It wasn't so much that he wanted to go on being with Luke, but he wasn't ready, yet, to be without him.

"All right," he said at last, "but I won't stay long."

The next morning, he was sorry he'd promised. His eyes felt a little better after he'd bathed them with icy water. They were still swollen, still stinging, but at least he could see.

Plodding behind Luke on the trail, he recognized a large boulder where he'd stopped on the way up to loosen a too-tight boot lace. He remembered how his father's pack had swayed, bumping the rock when he'd bent over to help him. They passed by the open place where Johnny had been so sure the two dark, circling forms above them were eagles, though his father had insisted they were ospreys. They passed the marsh where the horse was shot. Soon after they left the canyon, Luke turned from the broad trail into a narrow path that followed the river. He stopped where the trees were thickest and said, "Leave his load here."

"And have it stolen?"

"Here is not like town. I will make cache. No one will take."

He climbed high into a large tree and lashed the pack firmly to branches and trunk. Johnny painfully sat down, and when Luke had finished, painfully stood again to follow him.

Up and down they went, out of muskeg to low wooded slopes and from low wooded slopes to muskeg. When Johnny lagged behind, Luke urged him on, "Will be there soon."

At last he pointed ahead to where long swirls of water cut one sweep of land into many. "On other side of hills is wide water. You can see?"

"Not yet." Johnny struck out wearily at a cloud of midges hanging over him and shook his head. His eyes made everything bleary and he felt dizzy. Water and land glittered together and darkened as he sank down, crawled a few steps, and, clinging to Luke, made himself walk again.

Time passed in a blur of shore with nestling houses. Someone calling and the furious barking of dogs. Many hands lifting him. Lying still in darkness with cool wetness over his eyes. Sleeping. Waking. Hearing gentle talk he couldn't understand and sleeping again. Waking to the sound of rain. Sleeping. Waking, finally, and stretching to feel no hurt.

Johnny took the cloth from his eyes and let them follow the span of dark wooden rafters over his head. He could see! Smoke swirled through a hole in the roof and, as he watched it, he slowly realized that he would never see his father again. Turning on his side, he pressed his arms hard across his eyes. When he removed them, he saw Luke lying on a kind of sleeping shelf near him. The Indian boy smiled. Johnny smiled back. It was as though he were looking at someone he'd known a long time. "Let's get going," he said.

"First we have food."

They had venison and tea and a dried chewy lump of something that tasted good, like berries. Luke's father, a tall, quiet man, showed them the hide and horns of a mountain goat he had killed the day before.

"The horns we will make for spoons," Luke said. "I will show you."

His mother opened a carved and painted chest and stood by, smiling, as Luke spread out a collection of horn spoons, each cut in a different intricate pattern. Last he took out a white wool blanket, centered with an animal design and edged with pearly buttons.

"Killer-whale design," Luke told Johnny proudly. "The mama of my mama's mama weave it. Buttons come from old trade with Russians."

Johnny nodded. Luke's pride in his family and possessions made his own unbelonging more real than ever. Yet when the Indian boy suggested they look around the village before leaving, he couldn't say no.

Anyway, his eyes felt good, almost strangely so, as though, gradually, they were seeing more for his father than for himself. For what there was to see would have so greatly interested his father — the skin of the great black bear stretched on a frame to dry, two women working over a fresh skin to ready it for tanning or the long-handled netlike scoop that an old man was mending.

"That for salmon catching," Luke explained. "When salmon time come. Not now. Now, we go fishing for other fishes if you like."

"I can't, Luke. I have to go."

"Soon." Luke waved and called a greeting to some young men; then he led Johnny to a big square building. The two great poles that formed its entranceway were carved and painted with the heads of animals and birds with huge beaks, eyes, or teeth.

"Ceremonial house," Luke said.

"What's there?"

"Things sacred to tribe. Only *shaman* knows all."

"What's *shaman*?"

Luke looked at him as though he'd asked something he shouldn't have. "White man call *shaman* medicine man. Sometimes make fun of Indian." Then quickly changing the subject, "I have wish to show you other thing."

He led Johnny between several shake houses and into an old shed where skins were hanging. He stopped before a small pelt, fastened, fur inward, against the wood and said, "This one *mine.*"

"What kind is it?"

"Wolverine. Very valuable. Very beautiful." He told how he had snared it, how fierce wolverines were, how clever and difficult to catch. "It will buy fine thing. Of all things white men sell, there is one thing I wish for." He turned to Johnny, eyes bright and waiting.

"What?"

"Telescope."

"Oh." Johnny said, surprised.

"You know telescope?"

Johnny nodded, and Luke explained that he'd seen one for the first time at the mission school. Later he'd seen another at the Bee Kay Trading Post. Their value was much, he said, but so was that of a wolverine hide. "Very fine for hoods of parka. Will not freeze when wet."

"Yes, but what's so wonderful about a telescope?"

Luke frowned. "You look in one some time?"

Johnny nodded.

"It is not that I would lose gift of my people. The knowing of spirit of all creatures – knowing of his hunger, his speech, the ways of all his nights and days. I would have telescope for greater knowing. To go where *my* seeing cannot go, to bring far near. To show to me bird in nest, fox in den. Old men of tribe say they do not believe in such thing. When telescope is mine, they will see."

"My father had one once," Johnny said. He slowly walked away toward a row of big canoes lying along the shore.

Luke followed him. "You wish to catch fish?"

"Luke," he said as patiently as he could, "I have to go."

"Very late for starting today. We go tomorrow." He was grinning.

Annoyed but, in a way, relieved to put off having to go back to his father's world without him, Johnny sighed. "You'll go with me for sure then? You promise?"

Luke's eyes searched his. "You wish to go then, sure, we go."

Indians Know How to Live

5

LUKE'S CANOE was long and slim and had a whale's head carved and painted on the prow. "We make boats old way," he said. "Of cedar wood. Scorch hull with fire. Make splinters go. Rub all over smooth with sharkskin to leap fast over water."

Never had Johnny seen such clean, clear water. It broke around them like bubbled air as Luke pushed off. For a while they moved swiftly through it, then drifted as Luke rested his paddle and baited his hook.

Johnny, watching, did as Luke did and dropped his

line over the curved side of the boat. "What might we catch?"

"Halibut, cod, smelt. Not salmon yet. Salmon time is best one for my people."

"When's that?"

"Middle-of-sun-time, salmon come to us. Very many come to us, running."

Johnny, squinted at the shining water, and shifted his line. "You mean when they go upstream to spawn?"

"My people say salmon are race of beings like men. They live and feast in great house under sea. One time in year, they put on salmon flesh and come to us, that my people may have food. Good Indian must place salmon bones on water after eating, so beings can return to bottom of sea. Next middle-of-sun-time, they come again."

Johnny stared at him suspiciously. "If you believe that, you must be. . . ."

"What you believe?"

"When salmon are ready to spawn, they spawn. And that's all."

"What does it mean, *spawn*?"

"It means something like laying eggs. I read that when salmon are ready to do it, they leave the ocean. They find their own rivers and fight their way upstream to spawn where they were spawned. Then they die and the eggs grow to be fish and go back to the ocean. It's as simple as that."

Luke burst out laughing. "You think your salmon story not so magic as mine. You crazy. You know that?"

"Hey!" yelled Johnny. One minute he'd been smiling at Luke's dark, laughing slits of eyes, the next his line was taut and he was pulling hard.

"Halibut," breathed Luke. "Beauty halibut."

After that Johnny let himself drift with what was left of the day. Catching the fish had seemed to push him into a slow Indian dream. He ate with the others from a huge copper kettle. He watched sea gulls skittering overhead with shimmer in their wings and heard the slipping back and forth of water on the shore.

Young men and boys stood around talking. A few spoke in English of hunting or fishing or packing for white men. Others spoke their own tongue, teasing together. Later, with left-over sunset changing land and sky and sea to shining gold, the *shaman* came. He was shaggy-haired, and wore many necklaces and a wild-looking mask that was much bigger than his head.

"For dance," Luke explained. Then, as though hinting that he and Johnny might join in, "Dance very good medicine for sorrow."

"No, *thanks*. You go ahead if you want to."

The mention of sorrow was like being slapped awake. Johnny felt himself shiver as he had up there on the pass. As though the beat of the rawhide drums were merging with the awful sound of that wind. The leaping dancers with their weird animal masks, feathers, bear claws, bird beaks, and rattles made a panic in his mind and he longed to sob out and run.

Instead, he sat hugging his knees, to keep his shaking inside, and tried to feel contempt. Men and older boys acting like simpletons with all their stamping and leaping. Yet, turning finally to Luke, he had a very strange feeling that they weren't watching the same thing, that whatever Luke was seeing *must* mean something. He looked so pleased, so intent; and though he wasn't moving, it seemed as though some part of him might be out there, dancing with the others.

Later, as they lay on the sleeping shelf, side by side, Johnny asked Luke, "What was all that jumping around out there supposed to mean?"

"Mosquito dance. It tells story of mosquito, how they start."

"How did they?"

"When earth was young, cannibal giant, all the time ate people. People get mad, very mad, say to him, 'If you don't stop eating us, we kill you.' 'You kill me,' cannibal giant say back, 'you be sorry. For I not die.' He speak right, too." Luke chuckled softly. "They kill him and his spirit break into million tiny giants, many as sands on the shore. Mosquitoes. Cannibal mosquitoes."

Johnny grunted in disbelief.

"You do not understand? My people, long time ago, ask *why*. Why salmon come back, why bird fly, why mosquito eat man? Why? They make answers, best they can. Did not your people too, in youngness of time, ask why?"

"I guess so." Where were his people in ancient times when America was home only to Luke's people and other Indians? By the time the colonists came, men knew the world was round. But they *had* once thought you could sail off the edge of it. Once they'd thought the sun rose and set every day. He remembered studying a story at school. It was about a kid driving the sun chariot for his father, the sun god, Apollo. Maybe that was an old answer to a why. Why are some places hot? Why are some cold?

Light flickered from what was left of the fire at the center of the house. "What if your mother and father were dead?" Johnny asked suddenly.

"My sadness would be as yours," Luke said low. "You think Indian not feel as you?"

"I was just wondering."

"Only difference, I would not have as big worry as you. If my family all die, I have my family tribe. Indians take care of that good."

Johnny woke with sun in his eyes and the smell of cooking fish, but in his mind he was already on his way. The last miles covered, he saw himself aboard a ship, any ship, watching Alaska fade from his sight. He sighed, impatient to get started, wishing Luke would wake. He slapped at a buzzing close to his face, watched a mosquito settle on Luke's cheek and, unthinking, struck it.

Luke's eyes sprang open.

"Got him!" Johnny grinned at Luke's surprised look.

"Mosquito?"

"Sure," Johnny said, "big cannibal giant."

Luke's face crinkled with pleasure and, for a moment, both boys played, their arms flailing, as they punched and killed little black giants. Then Johnny, anxious to leave, rolled his wolfskin into his blankets and bent to lace his boots.

"Some day, when telescope is mine, you come to look with me?"

Johnny couldn't answer. He wanted to tell Luke he'd been swell; he wanted to thank Luke's mother for taking care of his eyes, the whole family for being kind to him. But he was afraid he'd cry and, anyway, he had to go. He threw his roll over his shoulder, calling good-by as he ran out the door.

"Wait. John-ee."

Luke caught up to him, blocking his way. "Maybe you stay when you hear new thing."

"Luke, I. . . ."

"Wait. I speak to you true. Indian knows how to live. Animals in hills and fish in sea make food for him always. Tribe makes brothers always. Hear me, John-ee. My papa speak to *shaman* that you have no papa, no mama. *Shaman* say you stay; he will make you one of my tribe. I will teach Indian ways to you."

Be an Indian? Couldn't Luke understand *anything*? "I couldn't do that," Johnny said quickly. "I *have* to go home."

"I have seen your sorrow. You have slept under my roof. As brothers, we dance, hunt, fish – what you like – to be happy again. All Killer-Whale people your friends."

Johnny walked by him, shaking his head.

"You do not wish . . . ?"

"Luke, listen. I wish to go home, that's *all* I wish. Anybody'd know that. What I *really* wish is that we'd never come to Alaska. I wish I had my father back, that's what I wish." Tears choked him. "So what's left but to go? Fast!"

Luke did not answer. He handed Johnny a handful of dried meat, then swift, tall, and secret-faced again, took the lead on the trail.

The cache where Johnny's father's belongings had been left was safe, though the branches covering it had been broken and pushed away. Luke pointed to a tear in the fold of the tent and to the wide-spaced claw marks on the trunk of the tree.

"Bear," he said briefly.

Johnny whirled to look behind him. Then feeling sheepish, he said, "I guess you're not afraid of bears."

"Anyone fool not to fear bear," Luke said, and shouldering the load, he set off again.

Behind him, Johnny thought how everywhere in this country there was something waiting to hurt you: bears, mosquitoes, snow slides, mountain passes. He was glad when he and Luke were back on the main trail again even though they often had to step aside to let gold seekers, burdened with equipment, pass.

Johnny asked one of the men if a boat had come in.

"Sure," he replied. "Pretty sure, that is. Came in on one yesterday. From Seattle. Poor beggar who was with me had his pack stolen last night. They'd steal the. . . ."

"Thanks. If there's a boat there, I have to get it."

Johnny hurried to catch up with Luke. As they neared the town, he said, "I'm going to make straight for the pier, Luke, to see if a boat's there and when it's going to sail. Will you take the stuff to the trading post for me?"

"You mean Bee Kay? Better you deal with Kirov."

"I will. I'll be right there. Soon's I find out." Johnny raced toward the waterfront his bedroll bobbing on his back.

A small ship lay out at anchor and several men were

loading a rowboat by the wharf.

"When does it go?" Johnny gasped.

"Within the hour, likely."

"I'm the captain," a small, red-faced man said. "What d'you want?"

"I want to go on it."

"To where?"

"San Francisco."

"Got the cash?"

"How much?"

"One hundred simoleons."

"Yeh." Johnny laughed.

He thought the captain was teasing until one of the men said, "Have a heart, Cap. He's only a kid."

"I'm interested in cargoes, not kids."

"I'll work, sir," Johnny said.

"Seventy-five dollars then, and you can work out the difference in the galley."

"I haven't got that much."

"What have you got?"

Johnny couldn't remember. That time in the tent at the top of the pass when he'd held the money in his hand seemed long, long ago. He dug in his pocket, pulled out his father's purse and showed its contents to the captain.

"Chicken feed. Forget it, kid," he said and started away.

Johnny rushed after him. "Please, I'll work hard. I

promise. Because I *have* to go."

The captain swung round. "What you running away from?"

"Nothing. I. . . ."

"If you've done wrong, been thievin' or something, I don't want you on my ship. Get out of my way now and stop botherin' me." He snapped an order at a sailor, stepped into the rowboat, and they pushed off.

"Listen, sonny." A shabby drunk man staggered up to Johnny. "If it's gold you need, you wanna go other way. Klondike. Tha's where gold is, boy. Nuggets big as marbles, yellow as butter . . . big as butter. . . ."

A Job

6

SICK AND DEJECTED, Johnny turned and walked along the shore, away from people, away from town. He righted a sand crab that had got turned on its back and watched it scuttle away. He watched lines of birds arrowing out of the south, where he longed to be. He crawled into a rotting rowboat that lay on the shore and saw the ship making ready to go. Black smoke puffed from her smokestacks and the sounds of shouting men reached him as the anchor was lifted.

When the whistles blew, he stood up. Not looking at the ship, he walked as slowly and sadly as a sleepwalker to the trading post and the one person in all the world who now seemed familiar to him.

But Luke was gone.

"I wanted to see him," Johnny explained to Mr. Kirov. "He must have known I wanted to see him."

"He waited for you quite a long while," Boris Kirov said. "Part of the time, in here, staring at a telescope he's taken a shine to, then outside, sitting on the steps. I understood he thought you were going on that ship that just pulled out. When she whistled, he left."

"I *have* to see him." Dimly aware of others in the store, the girl, for one, and a woman, Johnny leaned over the counter, almost shouting. "I wanted to thank him."

"Don't take on, lad, "Boris Kirov said, and for a moment Johnny listened to him. "The Indian boy told us of your trouble and it's surely a terrible and grievous thing you've been through. Mrs. Kirov and I and Elie here, are sorrier than we can say. If there's anything at all we can do. . . ."

"Excuse me but I have to catch him." Johnny tore out of the store and down the steps, searching both sides of the street as he ran. Before he reached the edge of town he knew it was hopeless. He was already winded and even if Luke didn't go his fastest – and why shouldn't he

– Johnny could never overtake him. Besides he suddenly realized he had no idea where Luke might go, back to his village or to be a packer again at the pass. He hadn't thought to ask him. He guessed he hadn't thought much about anything except himself.

Plodding back through town, he struck out furiously at a cloud of midges hovering near his face. From a gambling house came sounds of shaking dice and loud talk. A poor little donkey, loaded with two packs and a big man, shied as its hoof struck a bottle buried in the mud of the street. Filled with disgust, Johnny ducked and ran as two foolish women, dressed fancy as pictures, laughingly pretended to grab at him.

His stomach hurt with loathing of this place. By the time he reached the Bee Kay his head was whirling. Afraid he was going to be sick, he groped his way along the log walls to the back of the building. There behind a shed, he sank to his knees, head down and fists clenched.

When he looked up two big dogs were quietly watching him, a white one and the Kirov dog, Kiska. Johnny scrambled quickly to his feet and with heart pounding, pressed back against the building, ready to kick. The white dog backed away, barking. Kiska growled, and in a moment the girl, Elie, was there. "We told them to find you and take care of you and they did," she told Johnny.

"Big thing, finding me here," he said. "Right around

the corner." He moved away from her, brushing himself off.

She laughed that quick light way he'd noticed before and, almost at once, was serious again. "I don't know what I'd do either if it happened to me."

"If what happened."

"If. . . ." Tears filled her eyes and she couldn't finish.

She's just what I *don't* need, he thought, and to change the subject, asked if the white dog was hers too.

"Yes. His name is Booblick, which, I think, means something like little cake or cookie in Russian. He's not very little, of course, but he was when I got him." She was speaking slower, for a change. "Kiska's the dark one. He's an Eskimo dog and we haven't had him very long."

She bent to hug Booblick. "What are you going to do?"

"What do you think? Go home, naturally. As soon as I can earn some money." He heard his own cocky voice and was surprised. Then he remembered something. "When I was in your store that first time, your father offered me a job. You think he meant it?"

"Yes." She nodded solemnly. "Is your mother in San Francisco?"

"She's dead. But my aunt and uncle and cousins live there."

"Johnny, stay. Please." She smiled at him, pleading. "*Please.*"

"I'd never stay here," he said. "*Never.*"

"Why?"

"Because I hate it. That's why. I hate everything about it."

"Not every*body* though, huh? Or you wouldn't have been so upset about the Indian boy's leaving. Or run after him the way you did."

He shrugged, then walked around the building and up the steps into the store. The girl and the white dog followed him. Mr. Kirov was busy with two men. Johnny waited, his courage going.

"Mr. Kirov," he blurted out when the men left the store, "I want that job."

"What job?"

"Don't you remember?" He felt a burning in his eyes. "When I was here with my father? You asked if I wanted to work here. Well, I do."

Boris Kirov thoughtfully scratched his head. "For how long?"

"Till I can earn passage money home. Or, until some captain will let me work my way."

"If it's a place you need to stay until sailing time, then stay and welcome. We're glad to have you. But if it's a job you're asking for – well, no use teaching you the ropes to have you leave on the first ship. You can understand that. Just been through it with another fellow. I think I told you."

"Yes, sir, you did."

"How are you at arithmetic?"

"All right."

"You're young for hard work. And hard work, Johnny, is what some of it would be."

"I can do it."

"Maybe you can. If you weren't fairly hardy, I guess you wouldn't be standing here figuring on a job, not after what you've been through."

"If it hadn't been for Luke, I mightn't be."

"If you'd consider staying a while, say for the next three and a half months – through May, June, July, and part of August – while the gold seekers will be pouring in here, why then, at the end of summer, I'll buy your passage back myself, with a solid nest egg for good behavior thrown in."

"I couldn't stay that long." To Johnny the end of summer seemed as far away as the end of time. He wished the girl would stop staring at him.

"Look Johnny," Mr. Kirov said kindly, "you're exhausted. Why don't you take some time to rest and think things over? Go into the back room there. Show him, Elie. He'd better see it anyway, just in case. It goes with the job."

It was a small dark room with a bed, chair, braided rag rug, and a washstand and stove. It had a bookshelf with pegs under it for hanging clothes and a lamp bracketed to the wall.

Kiska stayed near the door but Booblick lay down and watched Elie. She was trying to raise the window shade. "It won't be so dark when the storm shutters are taken down," she said.

It was hard for Johnny to keep his mind on what she was saying. He was glad when she called out, "Wait a minute," and rushed from the room. Booblick followed her but the brown dog stayed. Johnny sat down and they eyed each other until Elie returned with her mother, a small blonde serious-looking woman.

"Go out now, Elie," she said, "and take Kiska with you."

"Do I have to?"

Her mother nodded firmly. She handed Johnny a cup of tea, placed a tray of sandwiches and fruit beside him and when they were alone, said, "Johnny?"

He looked at her.

"You're going to be all right. You'll find friends. Remember that." She touched his cheek. "You're going to be fine," she said and went out, closing the door behind her.

Johnny swallowed hard and reached for one of the

sandwiches of thick bread slices and meat. He devoured it and, surprised at how hungry he was, ate the other sandwich too. Leaving the dish of peaches, he drank the tea and lay back, his arms under his head, to think.

Johnny woke up, confused and chilly, in a room full of light. He looked around. Same washstand, lamp, and chair. Empty teacup and plate. Only the light was different. He could see outside. Someone had taken the storm shutters away.

He shivered and looked around for his bedroll. If he ever lost that wolfskin, he'd. . . . Where was it? Where, in fact were the other things, the ones Luke had brought. Had Mr. Kirov paid for them already, Luke taking his share? What if they'd been valuable?

He got up. What if they were worth enough, with what he had, to pay his passage? As he reached for the door, he caught a glimpse of himself in the mirror. He was dirty, his face chapped and peeling from wind and snowburn, his eyes red rimmed, his thick hair wild. He stared for a moment, startled by the change in himself, before bending over the wash basin. He scrubbed his hands and face, combed his hair, and went out.

Mr. Kirov was alone with Kiska. The dog growled.

"Kisk! Cut it out! You nervous around dogs?" he asked Johnny.

"A little."

"Yeh. They know lots of what goes on in a human's mind. Just never come at him sudden and he won't bother you."

"Is my pack here?"

"Yes, *sir*. Right there behind the counter."

"What about the supplies?"

"There, too."

"Are they worth something? Did you pay Luke half?"

"You mean the Indian? No, was I supposed to? He didn't say anything. Matter of fact, I haven't had a chance to look at the stuff. I'll do that right now. Do you want to help or haven't you made up your mind yet about working here?"

"No, sir, I haven't. But I'll know – I mean, as soon as I know what the things are worth, I'll. . . ."

"Let's hop to it then. You unload; I'll check 'em. Right off, I'll give you two dollars fifty cents each for the pick and shovel."

"Tent?"

"Ten dollars."

Johnny, thinking of a larger figure, said, "It's pretty good except for here where a bear clawed it."

"That won't keep it from being sold. But I appreciate your calling it to my attention. I'll still give you ten dollars."

Lovingly, Johnny handed over his father's clothes.

Socks, work pants, extra work shirt.

"Six dollars."

"Frying pan?"

"A dollar fifty. Coffee pot, the same." He looked rapidly over the odds and ends. "Five dollars for the lot. I want to give you a break. I'm paying you about what I can get for them. Hope it helps a little." He counted aloud, "Five, fifteen, twenty-one, twenty-four, twenty-nine. Twenty-nine even." He unlocked the money drawer under the counter. "Got something to put it in?"

"For mine but not Luke's. Half is his."

"I wouldn't know about that." He handed Johnny an empty tobacco sack and counted the money into it.

Johnny, who had been doing some counting himself, sighed deeply. The thirty he had, plus half of twenty-nine. . . . "I'd better take that job," he said.

"You sure you understand what it means? Work through to the middle of August and be paid, at that time, with your fare to Frisco and whatever extra I think you've earned. That's the contract."

"All right."

"Good." Smiling, he pressed Johnny's shoulder. "I'm proud to see a fellow fight his own way out of a corner."

It comforted Johnny to realize that his father might have said those very same words. "What do you want me to do now, Mr. Kirov?"

"Now! Why, it's practically bedtime. And you can call me Boris. Keep it easy."

In his room, Johnny unrolled his few possessions and put them away. Sitting up in bed, the wolfskin warm around him, he pressed out a piece of paper that his father had carried wrapped around a pencil and wrote: "Dear Aunt May and Uncle Bill – A terrible thing has happened. . . ."

He wrote what he had to say as fast as he could, finishing, "but don't worry about me. I'm working here for the present. Hope to see you before school starts. Love to all, Johnny."

For a long time he leaned against the window, watching the sky. Pink light filled it and fell over the earth. Right outside where neat garden rows had been furrowed, two small birds scratched, picking for seeds. They looked like the white-crowned sparrows he'd seen in California, the very same kind. Were they at home here or were they as lost and lonely as he?

The birds flew away and Johnny pushed down into bed with the blanket over his eyes. He couldn't get used to lightness at bedtime and wondered why Elie had bragged about it.

I wonder if I'll get to see Luke again, he thought suddenly.

Straight-Line Life

7

IN THE NEXT MONTH, gold seekers poured through the town by the thousands. Old-time prospectors came, and men who had never used a shovel in their lives. There were young men looking for adventure and vulture men, expecting to get rich off the others.

Tents and crude shelters were crowded into every vacant lot, between buildings, and along streets right down to the water's edge. Boarding houses, saloons, and gambling houses were wilder than ever.

All day long, day after day, as miners tramped in and

out of the store, Johnny worked, too busy to think. He replaced stock on the shelves from the storeroom, ran errands, and kept a lookout for the men about whom Boris had warned him, "They look as innocent as babies but they're as crooked as a dog's hind leg."

Johnny knew he was living his life in a straight line, leading only to home. Refusing to be interested in anyone or anything, he made a crude calendar, tacked it on the outside of the door of his room, and each morning grimly crossed off another day.

When he had free time, he explored one small section of town that seemed to turn its back on the rest: Mrs. Monahan's boarding house with its carefully tended young plants growing behind a white picket fence; the Appleton Lumber Yard, a tall shed over two great piles of logs, with Mr. Appleton usually there, working near his sawhorse; the neat two-story house where the schoolteacher lived with his family; two other small houses with clean swept porches; and Mr. Jack's saddle, feed, and grain store. The people Johnny saw there, who nodded or spoke to him, were the ones who most looked or acted like his aunt and uncle and their friends.

Not that he was forgetting how kind and thoughtful the Kirovs were. Or Luke, who had been good to him in that special way. Or even Elie, who was always going out of her way to cheer him up. In fact she was pesky about it, following him around and talking, always wanting him to walk or go for a ride with her in her dog cart.

"Stop buzzing around me like a mosquito," he told her once. She hadn't liked it, which was understandable, considering that the mosquitoes and black flies, swarming now in clouds, were the most bothersome things around.

She pestered him about the dogs too, trying to get him and them to like each other. Booblick wasn't so bad, but Kiska growled every time Johnny came near. Well, let him growl, their feelings were mutual. Except that sometimes, he seemed to get his feelings for the great brown dog and his wolfskin a little mixed up, as though he wished the aliveness of one could be in the other.

At least he didn't get animals mixed up with people the way Elie did. She was pretty idiotic that way, insisting that even the wild ones had feelings like people. She said that if you were nice to them, speaking respectfully and minding your own business, they'd be nice to you. Naturally, she said, they had to defend themselves when they were threatened. No wonder her family wouldn't let her go walking very far alone. And, so far, he'd made sure he was too busy to go with her.

Boris was always telling him not to work so hard. "Take time to listen," he'd say. "Some very interesting people come in here. Hardly a day passes that I don't learn something I didn't know before."

Johnny, busy piling up soap or matches or candles, rarely answered. To him, most of the talk in the store was the kind he never wanted to hear again, blown-up stories of gold strikes made or to be made. The only men he was interested in were those on their way out — a Nebraska farmer, a Colorado schoolteacher, a brakeman for a Texas railroad — all sensible enough to be going home.

The only time he asked for time for himself was when the ships were in. He'd stand around the wharf, longing to be one of those being rowed out to the ships in small boats to go aboard. Sometimes, when Elie and the dogs hadn't tagged along with him, he'd talk to members of the crews. Once he talked to a captain who offered to let him work his way back.

Funny, he thought, to get that offer now, after he'd made his promise to Boris. If he had to work, though, nobody could be better to work for. Boris even seemed to understand about his missing his father, though Johnny hadn't realized it for a while. Not till the time when Boris had misunderstood his brooding over the telescope.

"Your father wouldn't have wanted you to mope, Johnny," he'd said.

But for once, Johnny hadn't been moping. He'd been remembering that Luke's face had worn the same look when he'd invited him to belong to his tribe as it had when he'd spoken of the telescope.

He'd been so deep in those thoughts that he was startled when Boris spoke to him. "I know," he said after a moment.

"Your father wanted to come to Alaska, didn't he?"

"More than anything."

"All right then. He died doing what he wanted to do. Any man has a right to do that. As for you, he might have wanted you to see a big, new land. Few kids have that chance – to live in majestic, clean, new country."

"Clean!" Johnny snorted. "With all the cheating and stealing and. . . ."

"Patience, Johnny." Boris held up his hand. "It takes patience. It is a rough land but it's also a great one. It'll smooth out. Stay around and you'll see."

"Not me."

"I thought you might change your mind, decide to stay."

"Not for anything, I wouldn't." He turned quickly away, feather-dusting a lantern, the oil lamps, a pile of snowshoes.

"Liking you the way we do, I thought you might come to like us." A gust of wind blew the door open, scattering the papers Boris had been working on.

Johnny scrambled to pick them up. "You said I could go in August. You promised you'd give me the fare."

"You think I mightn't keep my word?"

Johnny tried not to show his trembling. "I'm not sure," he spoke softly, then stopped, sorry about the silence he'd made.

"Have I been unfair to you in any way?" Boris asked at last.

"No. No, sir. Not to me. You've been great to me and fair to the miners too. Very fair. I've noticed that."

"What then, exactly, are we talking about?"

"The Indians."

"Oh." Boris smiled as though relieved. "Don't you worry about the Indians. They'll get wise."

Johnny shook his head. "But if you're fair — those fish, for instance, the oily ones with the wicks pulled through that the miners use for candles. . . ."

"Oolaken fish?"

"Yes. You give the Indians five or six cents each for them in trade and sell them to the miners for half a dollar. Is that fair?"

"Sure. The Indians come here to trade. I trade." He rumpled Johnny's hair, laughing. "That's what a trading post is all about. You know that."

Johnny shook his head.

"Ah, come now."

"I understand about the trading part. What I don't understand is why one man can get more in trade than another."

"If you mean, why does an Indian get less, well, I'll tell you." He spoke impatiently. "He expects it. Settles for it." More gently, he added, "You and your Indians. That Luke friend of yours never did come back here, did he?"

"No."

"And that matters?"

Johnny glared at him. "Yes, it does. I told you how I feel about him and his people."

"Cool off. You want him to show up. I hope he shows up."

Johnny wished he could agree with Boris about his business methods with the Indians, but he couldn't. He tried figuring out what his father might say if he could talk to him about it but that didn't help much. The answers he got were either too much like his own, siding with the Indians, or too much like Boris's, that business is business, not only in Alaska but everywhere.

Late in June, Elie watched him mark one more day off the calendar with his usual flourish. "I hate the way you act about that old calendar," she said.

"Too bad."

"All you think about is going away."

"That's right."

"To where there are horse cars and paved streets."

"That's right."

"And someone to take care of you."

"I don't need anyone to take care of me."

"Hmmmm." She smiled her maddening smile.

"You're a fine one to talk."

Instantly her face was soft. "I know."

He hated the way she agreed with him sometimes, as though she were sympathizing. He watched two great flies bumbling around in the sunlight against the window, then walked away from her, out the door, and onto the porch. Kiska, lying near the top step, ignored him.

A gust of wind whipped Johnny's hair and lifted clouds of dust from the dried-out mud and fragments of horse droppings. Kiska snapped at a fly and flicked his ears at others. Johnny squashed a mosquito on his hand.

"Johnny?" Elie came up behind him. "I should think as long as you're here, you'd like to see what the country's like now that it's summer. Away from town, I mean. We could take a walk." At the sound of the word walk, both dogs stood alert, ears up, tongues out, watching her. "Look, they want to go too. Why don't we take the dog cart?"

"I've seen enough."

"Not the beautiful part." She came right up to him. "You never look! Forget-me-nots, wild roses. . . ."

"Flowers," he scoffed. "What about the poor guy they brought into town yesterday? Half his face clawed away by a bear."

Elie covered her face with her hands. "Did you know

a bear killed Speed?" She barely lifted her head. "He was another dog I had. I was with him when it happened. But I bet bad things happen to people and dogs in San Francisco too."

"You were with him?"

"Yes. We were running, playing in a field back of here. The bear was round and black and only half-grown – and he was rolling, like a puppy in a bed of blue wild-flowers. Bears never come that close any more."

"What'd you do?"

"Walked away. But Speed wouldn't. I guess he thought he had to protect me and he made the bear nervous. If you make wild things nervous, then, naturally, they act wild."

"And I suppose if you bow low and shake hands with them, they love it."

She frowned at him. "People live to grow up here as much as they do anywhere else. My mother and father did and I'm going to, too. I'm going to grow up and teach."

"Where?"

"Here. Where do you think? Here, where they need teachers. And where I can have my animals and birds and flowers and northern lights and sunshine at night." She was half laughing, half singing now. "And trees and clear water and mountains all around."

"Those mountains killed my father. Don't forget that."

"Oh, Johnny, they didn't. People die because . . . because. . . ."

"Because what?" He glared at her and she glared back. "Go ahead," he insisted. "You know so much. Because what?"

"Because it's part of being alive," she said.

"What's so being alive about dying?"

"How do I know? Only you *do* have to be alive to die, don't you? What if you never got a chance to be alive at all? Did you ever think of that, Johnny Clemens? If you don't want to be alive, then don't be. Don't ever use your eyes or be glad or, oh all right!" she said when he sneered. "At least I have more sense than to go around saying that mountains kill people. As though they could shoot guns at you or poisoned arrows or push a person off a cliff or something!"

He had never seen her so angry before. For the first time, *she* walked away from him. Her back was straight, her skirts swinging. Watching her, Johnny almost smiled.

The Little Foxes

8

THAT NIGHT Johnny dreamed of Luke, something about him and bear magic. Something that he couldn't remember in the morning except that he woke with a good feeling about it. He thought he felt a little the way he had before his father's death, half-expecting to see the flowered wallpaper of his San Francisco room when he opened his eyes.

And he felt like talking. At breakfast, he asked Boris if he'd ever met a bear. Boris, nodding, gave a short laugh.

"One time," he said, "river fishing, I got a strong feeling that I was being watched and followed. The feeling worried me all through the morning and then I saw him. Great brownie he was, out in the clear by the water, a hundred yards away. I'm telling you, my hair stood straight up. Instead of man stalking bear that bear was stalking man."

"What happened?'

"I'm alive to tell the story, aren't I? Might not have been if I hadn't played dumb and kept right on going, fast."

"You know what that reminds me of Boris?" Mrs. Kirov asked. "Remember when cousin Ida was here from the states? While I was still teaching?" She handed Johnny his oatmeal, "We were walking to the schoolhouse. I was talking and didn't notice a bear watching us, not ten feet from the trail. But Ida did and before I knew what she was doing, she threw him our lunch. 'To quick-satisfy his appetite and keep him away from us,' she said. We barely had time to reach the schoolhouse and pull the door latch behind us before his majesty, the bear, was there. Having snacked on our lunch he was looking for more."

Elie giggled.

"What'd you do?" Johnny asked.

"Cowered behind the stove while he shook the door. We thought it would surely fall in. The whole building rocked. Then, suddenly, all was still. When I finally got courage to creep to the window, there wasn't a sign of him. Later, some of the big boys took their guns, looking for him. But they didn't find him."

"And I'm glad," Elie said.

"His claw marks are still plain on the schoolhouse door."

"Can I see them?"

"Of course. Elie will show you."

Elie shrugged. "He doesn't want to see them. He doesn't want to see anything. He said so."

"Would it be all right with you, Boris?" Johnny asked.

"Sure. Go after lunch. Taking the dog cart, Elie?"

"No. It's a bother on the trail."

"Take both dogs, in any case. *Both*. Do you hear me?"

After lunch, Johnny sat on the trading-post steps, waiting for Elie. He frowned up at the sky where black clouds were knocking out the sunlight then looked down to see a tall young Indian walking toward him. He had a bundle on his back and came swinging along as Luke would have done. Johnny sighed. It wasn't Luke.

"Do you know anyone named Luke? Chilkat Tribe?" Johnny asked him.

He smiled, looking puzzled, shook his head, and walked into the store.

Johnny wondered if the Indian would be smiling after his trade was completed. Was it furs he was carrying? If so, Boris would be especially glad to get them. He thought of going in, so that Boris would be reminded of their talk. But just then Elie came with both dogs.

"Here," she said, a leash in each hand. "Which will you take?"

"You joking?" he asked her. "Better ask them which will take me."

"They have to if I say so. Kiska, go with Johnny."

Kiska didn't move.

"Here, take his leash."

Johnny did, thinking that if he'd known he'd have to lead that dog he wouldn't have said he'd go. He pulled and Kiska stood firm.

"*Speak* to him, Johnny."

Booblick, eager to go, was pulling Elie on ahead as Johnny muttered to Kiska, "Come on."

Kiska didn't move.

"Come on, Kisk," Elie sang out and the dog caught up to her, and Johnny with him.

"Why do they have to wear harnesses just to take a walk?" he asked.

"So they won't scare anything away."

"Like bears?"

"No, silly. Like deer. Even a moose, maybe. Or birds."

It didn't take long to reach the school and see the claw marks on the door. Standing there, the sun palely shining again and mosquitoes buzzing around, Johnny tried to imagine the bear. "How tall was he?"

"Up!" Elie ordered Booblick. "Up!" until he was standing on his hind legs against the door. "Much taller than that. Now, I suppose you're scared to do anything but rush right back."

He hated the way she seemed to read his mind. "What else is there to do?"

Her eyes darkened as she studied him, then they blazed blue again. "I know the very thing. Let's go. Kisk? Booblick?"

The dogs strained on their harnesses, yipping with pleasure until she shushed them. They cut over a hill, the town still within view, until they came out on a wide much-used trail.

Johnny recognized it at once. "Isn't this the way to the Chilkoot? What are we doing here?"

"We're only going along a little piece of it," she said, all smiles. "And I hope something's still where I think it is, where I saw it last year."

He wondered if she knew where she was going. Just like her with her wacky ideas about animals to try to feed them sugar out of her hand. Johnny slowed down to look behind him and Kiska jerked on the leash. The dog turned to look at him, ears up, as if to ask, What's worrying you, boy? At least, Johnny thought, he isn't snarling at me. Or trying to get away. Kiska was really smart. Pretty too, Johnny decided. His fur, right now, shone as fine as the wolfskin.

"Let's go, Kisk," Johnny said, trying it, and when it worked he felt like calling out to tell Elie.

She was right. The country was beautiful right now. Even the blue-green, white-topped mountains looked peaceful. Johnny had a flash of good feeling. The bog, so ugly when he and his father had passed it, was now covered with green plants and beautiful long-stemmed lavender flowers. A meadow waved with sun-catching pink grass, and another was white with something Elie called Alaska cotton.

There were wild roses everywhere, bigger than his aunt could ever imagine, with petals like red and pink tissue paper. And forget-me-nots! Wait till he got home and tried to tell Aunt May that the kind of flowers she tended so carefully in her little garden, grew *wild* in Alaska. Without thinking Johnny touched Kiska's fur, then touched it again and ran his hand softly along the dog's back.

"Hurry, Johnny."

He caught up with Elie as she moved from the trail to a clump of fir trees. "We'll leave the dogs here," she said, winding and tying Booblick's leash around one of the trees.

"Why?"

"You'll see. Here, I'll tie Kiska."

"I'll do it."

"Tight, then. They don't like to be left but it won't be for long."

"I thought your father meant us to stay with the dogs."

"We are. Practically." She spoke to the dogs, telling them to be good. "We'll be right back so *shush,*" she told them firmly. "Johnny, walk right behind me. Step as softly as you can."

She led him beyond the trees, across a stretch of slippery shale and loose, clinky rocks. "Shhh," she whispered, then, finger to her lips, she ducked down, pulling him with her.

"See?" She grinned, pointing.

"What?" he whispered.

"Up there, on the bank, where the bush is moving. Foxes. Their den is there. See them?"

For an instant, confusing foxes, bears, and wolves in his mind, he hardly knew what to look for.

"Johnny, do you see? One moved!"

He saw red of fur against gray of rock. There were two animals. One was almost hidden by the bush.

"They see us, too," Elie whispered. "Look, down there, almost in front of us. Little ones, playing. Two of them, no three. Four. Oh, Johnny!"

The young foxes were romping like puppies. Four fat, reddish balls of fur, chasing, tumbling, biting each other. One left the others, started down the slope and stopped, his firm little body tense with listening. The parent foxes moved into plain sight as though calling him back, while the other three young ones scampered up the rocks toward them. The kit continued downwards, stopping again less than six feet from where Elie and Johnny were crouched.

"Come, little honey," crooned Elie and it did, two steps closer. Johnny could see the light in the tips of its fur, the small curved-up line of its mouth, even the clearness of its questioning yellow-gray eyes.

A large bird flew over, so close they could hear the sound of its wings. The fox froze. The parent foxes paced back and forth, worried about their young one.

Elie clicked her tongue softly and held out her hands. It lifted one foot to come and was standing like that, undecided, when a great yip went up from the tied up dogs. The little fox swung around, fell over itself, rolled, clambered up, rolled again, got its footing, and turned, accusingly, to stare at them. Just exactly like an angry roly-poly baby, thought Johnny, and he burst out laughing.

The little one shook himself and, standing firm, used his hind foot to scratch behind his ear. Still looking at them, he seemed to twist his little mouth into a smile, and Elie and Johnny shook with laughter. The dogs yipped again, and the little fox, taking his time, ambled back to his family.

"I guess we'd better go now," Elie said. "Wasn't that wonderful? Seeing foxes where they live and acting so natural and everything?"

Before he could answer she squealed, "Johnny!"

He whirled. "What?"

"I just this second realized something. You were laughing!"

"You don't need to scare me to death."

"But you did."

"Anything wrong with that?"

"Not one single thing."

The way she said it made him feel funny, as though he could laugh again, easily, any time he felt like it. It made him feel funny in another way too. As though he could like her a lot if he'd let himself.

The wind had come up and was wailing, mean as witches, when they got back to the yipping dogs. "Idiots," Elie told them, "acting as though we've been gone for weeks."

Johnny untied Kiska, waiting for a growl. None came. "Elie?"

"Yes?"

"Do you know where the trail to the Indian village turns off this one?"

"I've never been there but I think it's somewhere between here and the canyon. Some of the children in our school walk all that long way and back every day."

"I have a feeling it starts near here. Could we go on, just a little way to find out?"

"All right. Only it looks like it may rain any minute."

Almost at once, it started to rain hard, and Elie said they'd have to go back. Johnny stared ahead through the haze, trying to see the turn-off. Then as Kiska pulled at him to follow Elie, he turned and headed back toward the town.

An old man, the usual pick and shovel sticking out of his pack, tramped past them.

"You kids been gold-seeking, too?"

"No sir."

"Ever seen the Chilkoot?"

"Yes," Johnny said.

"Is she a stinker?"

When Johnny nodded the old man gave a grunt of satisfaction. "Good. Something to brag to the grandchildren about when I get back." As he moved on, the wind whipped his hat off, hurtling it backwards. Johnny caught it and ran to return it.

"Good luck," he said, surprising himself.

Another Cheechako

9

When Johnny and Elie reached home, they tied the dogs in their shed and entered through the back way. Elie with Johnny behind her tiptoed along the hall, planning to startle her parents by shouting "Hello!" right behind them as she often did. But instead she stopped abruptly at the doorway of the store.

Her parents were alone and Boris's voice was loud. "All right then, Elena, think what you will. I run an honest business. When I trade, I'm going to do it fairly but also as much to our advantage as I can."

"Fairly!"

"*Your* folks were the missionaries. Mine were only *ordinary* humans. I don't take anything away from the Indians. I make them an offer, take it or leave it. Is it my fault if they're too dumb to catch on?"

Mrs. Kirov sighed deeply. "Boris, they're not dumb. Not even a little bit. They're not, and you know it." Johnny felt Elie shiver beside him as her mother went on. "They may not know yet the real values of their goods to white men. Or of dealing for white men's goods in white men's ways. They know values well enough – of cedar bark and blankets and furs – when trading with other Indians. These otter skins are beauties, Boris, so can't you. . . ." She started to lift one and saw the children. "Oh," she cried, "you're soaked."

Boris turned. "About time you're here. Where have you been?" he roared.

"Remember the fox den, Papa?" Elie said it, smooth as cream. "The one you and I found last summer? It's still there and a family of foxes and. . . ."

"What were you thinking of? To go that far without me?"

She laughed. "As though the dogs weren't with me. And Johnny."

"Johnny's a *cheechako* and a young one at that." Boris lowered his voice, speaking sternly as though Johnny weren't standing there dripping and miserable. "You think he's already as smart in the wilds as an Indian?"

Elie giggled. "Oh Papa, one minute you call Indians dumb and the next you call them smart. You'd better make up your mind."

"Upstairs!" He bellowed and she went slowly, shaking the wetness out of her hair.

"Change your clothes right away," her mother called after her, then, "Wait, I'll help you. You change yours too, Johnny," she said as she passed him.

Johnny waited. "You need me for anything first, Boris?" he asked at last.

Boris looked up as though surprised that he was still there. "See the foxes?"

"Yes, sir. Six of them. A whole family."

"Pretty sight, eh?"

Johnny nodded and Boris went to the counter. He shook out one of the new skins, dropped it and, sighing deeply, rubbed his hand over his eyes.

"My womenfolk don't understand this business." He spoke sadly, his big shoulders drooping. "Never will and won't try to. You know how women are." And, when Johnny didn't answer. "That's right. I forgot. You don't understand either."

That night, as he got ready for bed, Johnny puzzled over Boris. How could someone who seemed so sure and strong act so hurt and lonely and put upon? He was sure Boris meant well. Anyway, he hated to see him so troubled. Perhaps he should try to keep his mouth shut about things they didn't agree on. He could never really go along with the way Boris dealt with the Indians, but he could, at least, for the rest of his time here, try to keep quiet about it. He kicked off his boots and sighed. Thank goodness there was less than a month to go.

Sitting on his bed and looking out the window, he was glad he was sticking it out, earning his way. What would it be like, he wondered, to be living like other kids again? Playing Kick-the-Can instead of looking for foxes, going to a school with no bear scratches on the door, and walking on a firm sidewalk instead of loose boards over dirt.

He thought of the letter from Aunt May that had reached him the week before. How she'd called him her little Johnny and talked about taking care of him again. As though he were no older than his little cousins. Who did she think was taking care of him now, he wondered. He could almost hear her talking. *Put your rubbers on, Johnny. Did you wash your ears? Here, let me sew on that button, this minute, before you lose it. How do you expect to grow, picking at your food like that? Come on now, clean your plate.*

Tears blurred his eyes. It was as though Aunt May's face, so kind and worried over his skinniness, was right there before him. Even so, all that stuff she always fussed about was going to seem pretty silly to him at first, after these months of living practically like a man.

Was he really so different, bigger and older in his ways? Or did he just feel that way? Would Aunt May and Uncle Bill notice the difference? Would Luke, if they should meet again? If the turn-off to Luke's village was right beyond where he'd walked today, it would be simple enough to take the time to go there. He could thank Luke and give him his money. Maybe Luke would write to him when he was back in San Francisco. If he *could* write. At least Johnny could ask him.

He yawned, tightened his wolfskin, and lay back, watching a flight of birds in the golden twilight outside his window. They turned in the wind and settled, fluttering in the waving branches of a fir tree. They looked like fancy ornaments, arranged there to stay, yet in a moment they were off again, heading south in his direction. Home. If only he could be there as quickly as they would be.

A week later, at breakfast, Elie announced that she'd seen a newly arrived ship from the window of her room. "It's huge, all masts and sweeping sails. Want to go meet it, Johnny?"

Johnny looked at Boris, who nodded his head. "Go along."

It was very early morning, but already the tent dwellers were bent over their open fires. The air was heavy with the smell of frying bacon and sourdough pancakes. Some miners were already folding their tents to leave. One young man saluted the sun as it blazed through a silver cloud. "There's the sign," he called to his partner. "Let's get along."

A few called out to Elie and Johnny as they passed. One, a huge, ugly-looking man, told Elie it was a long time since he'd seen a pretty young girl. "You're a sight for sore eyes," he said, "particularly in a hell hole like this."

Johnny poked Elie to make her go on, then teased her. "See what he thinks of your town."

Elie ran ahead, her blue scarf whipping behind her.

Johnny caught up to her at the pier.

A schooner lay out in the harbor. Its sails were being furled. Three seamen climbed down a ladder over the side, jumped into a boat, and rowed toward them. Oars flashing, it came faster and faster, as though impatient to get there. As soon as it touched shore, a young man, his wild hair blowing, jumped out, rope in hand.

"Tie it up," the oldest of the three sailors yelled at him, "and mind you stay where we can find you when we're ready to go back."

"You want to go back, row yourselves back," the young man called after them. He grinned up at Elie and Johnny as they looked down at him from the jetty. "Hey, you two. Where can I find something besides potatoes and hardtack to eat?"

"At Mrs. Morgan's," Elie said. "She has a restaurant. Or maybe you'd like a boarding house?"

"I would rather have ham and eggs and good honest bread. Can you show me to them?"

Giggling, Elie took the lead as Johnny fell in step beside the sailor. "That's a fine ship you came on."

"That it is. The *Davy M*. A staunch friend and true. Though I am being urged by a couple of the crew to forsake it for the goldfields. With a sackful of nuggets, I could buy my own ship, go where I want to go, do what I want to do." He looked at Johnny, a great grin splitting his face. "Well, anyway, hello."

"Well, anyway," Elie laughed back at them, "welcome to Alaska."

"Thank you. And how is Alaska?"

"Ask her." Johnny nodded toward Elie. "I hate the place."

"What? And me thinking I might stay?"

"If you're hungry," Elie said, "here's Mrs. Morgan's."

"Mrs. Morgan, prepare yourself," he said and bowed to Elie. "Thanks again."

"You're welcome, *cheechako*."

"I'm welcome, what?"

"*Cheechako*."

"No savez cheechako," he called after them. "But my name's Bud. Starvin' Bud Riley."

"I'd like to sail back with a fellow like that," Johnny said.

Elie pretended not to hear him. "Remember how mad you got that time I called you *cheechako*?"

He grinned and slapped a mosquito on her arm. "And a sourdough, I'll never be."

"Don't you ever think of one single, solitary thing but leaving?" Without waiting for an answer, she rushed away, cutting around two arguing miners to do it. Chin up, she walked quickly by the saloon to the Bee Kay and up the steps.

The way she did that gave him a funny feeling, almost as though he were missing her already. The same feeling came again as Kiska, lying just outside the store door, looked up at him.

"Hello, fella," he said as Kiska's wolflike eyes studied him. He longed to pet that great head as easily as Elie did but couldn't quite make himself do it. "Remember me?" he said low and half-teasing. "We took a walk together."

He was sure there was a quiver along the shining fur but the tail didn't move. Kiska lowered his head to his paws and Johnny went on into the store.

Indian Cheater

10

Boris was helping two customers with a pack. They were a middle-aged man and his wife, dressed alike in blue plaid shirts, canvas pants, and boots. Watching them leave, Boris put an arm around Johnny's shoulders and shook his head.

"What some men will let their wives do," he said.

"She probably made him bring her with him."

Boris laughed. "Give her three or four hours on the Chilkoot and she'll wish she was back in the kitchen. Want to fill that bean barrel? It's getting low." And, as

Johnny started to the storeroom, "Check the tea and blackstrap molasses while you're there."

When Johnny came back, lugging a bucket of beans, Boris was busy outfitting some young men. Johnny poured the beans in a rattling stream into the barrel and replaced the lid. So that he wouldn't forget to report that they were short on tea, he scribbled "10 T." on a page of the open stock book on the counter.

He looked up as the store door opened to let in a shaft of sunlight and a tall young man. He was an Indian with a rolled skin in his hand, and he looked like Luke. Johnny's heart gave a leap as the Indian went at once to the telescope.

"Luke!" he yelled and dashed to him, grinning. "I thought you'd never come." He caught Luke's arm, wanting the Indian's surprised look to turn to pleasure. "More than almost anything, I've wanted you to come," he said.

Luke's face broke into a smile. "I think that day you go away. Quick, like you say."

"The captain wouldn't take me. I've been working here. I'm going soon, though, and I've been worrying I wouldn't see you. I guess you think if I wanted to see you so much, why didn't I come to your village?"

Luke nodded, his face listening and solemn. "Maybe you still scared of something."

Johnny laughed and changed the subject. "Listen

Luke. You didn't get your share of money from our pack. Fourteen dollars and fifty cents. Come on to my room."

"Boris," he called, "Luke's here."

Boris turned from his customers, his voice amused. "So I gathered."

"I'll be back in a minute."

"Take your time."

Johnny felt good having Luke in the room where he'd so often thought of him. He insisted Luke take the only chair. Then he counted out Luke's money and gave him the tobacco sack to put it in. After that he just sat on the bed, grinning. "Well," he said, "you been all right?"

Luke, sitting very straight with the rolled skin across his knees, nodded. "You been, also?"

"Sure. Only. . . ." He went to the window and waved toward the mountains. "You ever been back there?"

"Up Chilkoot? Many times."

"Where my father – I mean where we left him?"

"One time there. Where was snow, flowers now are very many. Grow up in bloom between stones."

"Oh." The thought of going up there sometime no longer seemed so frightening to him. In fact, if he were going to stay here, he'd probably ask Luke to go with him some day. "I've never seen northern lights like those that night," he said.

"They cannot show so bright in the light nighttime of

summer. Stay for winter darkness and you see them again, good."

"I can't. But Luke, I sure do thank you and your family for your goodness to me. How's that special fur of yours? That it?"

Luke grinned and patted his bundle. "Ready for trade. With telescope, from long way, I will see cow moose and young separate from water. See elk and caribou separate from forest. Also things like I tell you before. Come back with me. I show you."

"You come with *me*. See *my* town. Hills and bay and big buildings and fire engines."

"I be the scared one there."

They sat for a moment smiling at each other; then Luke stood up. "Now, I wish to talk to Mr. Kirov."

"I'll go with you," Johnny said.

Boris was making an entry in his record book, and Luke went right to him. "I have very fine wolverine skin," he said.

"Wolverine? Let's see it."

Luke unrolled and shook out the skin. He spread it flat on the counter where every separate yellow, white, and brown hair of it seemed to ripple and shine.

Boris gave a small grunt of surprise but his face was without expression as he turned the skin over and closely examined it.

"It's a beauty, isn't it, Boris?" Johnny said at last.

"I will exchange to you for telescope," Luke said.

"Oh, you will!" Boris barked his trader's laugh. "That telescope's worth forty dollars."

Luke looked straight at him. "The fur also."

"I'll give you twenty dollars in trade for it."

Luke shook his head.

"How about a gun?" Boris said. "That's more use to you than a telescope. Or what about a couple of those heavy, new-style bear traps? Show them to him, Johnny."

"He especially wants the telescope," Johnny said.

"Show him the traps."

Johnny stiffened with anger and hurt. He wanted to shout, "I won't" but the words wouldn't come. What if Boris got mad at him and broke their contract? What if, in one crazy, mixed-up minute like this, he should lose all he'd worked for? He remembered Luke's face when he'd first talked of the telescope. How it had changed from a closed man's face to a boy's happy one. Still he did not speak.

Luke broke the silence. "I have no wish for bear trap."

Boris reddened. "A two-man saw, then. With a lantern and canned stuff thrown in for good measure."

"Telescope," Luke said.

"Offer him money," Johnny blurted to Luke. "You know, the money I just gave you. *And* the fur."

Luke shook his head. His face was closed and secret again. "Mr. Kirov know well, fur is worth more than telescope."

"Listen here, Indian kid!" Boris blazed. "Are you trying to tell *me*?"

Luke's eyes didn't move from Boris's flushed and angry face.

"Go on," Boris said. "Get out!"

Luke rolled up the skin. Silently, without looking at either of them, he walked out of the store.

Boris stalked to the door and banged it shut. "Just who?" he demanded, "does he think he is?"

Johnny's fury broke loose. "Cheater!" he cried.

"Listen. . . ."

"You are! You know you are! You told me it was the Indian's fault if he didn't get a fair trade. That he should wise up. But you didn't mean it, did you? Luke wises up and what happens? You get mad and yell at him. He's a Tlingit Indian and proud of it, that's who he is! He came here to make an honest trade for a telescope he wants more than anything. And he's going to have it!" Johnny's voice broke around the lump in his throat. "Because I'm going to give it to him and you can't stop me."

"Johnny!" It was Elie, standing white-faced with her mother on the stairs.

Johnny lowered his voice. "You can charge it against

me, Boris. From what you owe me." Almost choking with tears, Johnny grabbed the telescope and its case from the shelf, hugged them inside his denim jacket, and ran to the door. Kiska stood there whining.

"Get away," he said to the dog.

"Johnny! Wait!" Mrs. Kirov called.

"I wish you hadn't made me, Boris. I wish. . . ." He wrenched the door open, closed it quickly behind him, and ran down the street.

He ran until his breath ached in his throat, out of town and on to the miner's trail. He tore by mountainbound prospectors who called after him, "What's your hurry, kid?"

Panting and sweating, he stopped for a minute to put the telescope in its case. He wished he'd left with Luke or that Luke hadn't moved so fast. Now he'd have to walk in wild Alaska alone.

As he turned off the main trail and came to the bear tree, an end-of-the-world feeling swept through him. With summer sunlight splashing, warm through the trees, he shivered.

He thought suddenly, here I am trying to catch up to Luke when he might still be in town. Perhaps he had some other errand there and if I wait he might come. He sat down, away from the tree, careful to stay alert.

Even if Luke didn't come, some other Indian might. If

he knew Luke and was going to his village, he could deliver the telescope, and Johnny could go back to the store. But could he go back? Would Boris let him? As clearly as though he were looking through a telescope much more powerful than the one he carried, he saw that door closed to him. Behind it, he imagined the hurt, accusing looks of the Kirovs.

He waited a long time while the whole miserable business went back and forth in his mind. He was hungry too, and he realized that supper time must have long passed. Here, where daylight went on for hours, you couldn't tell the time by the color of the sky. There would be some darkness between now and morning though and he didn't want to be caught in it. He was all by himself and he'd better face it. Wearily, he started to walk.

He thought how it might be if Kiska were with him. Friendly or not, they would be company for each other. He tried to ignore the unfamiliar sounds of the forest. His notions of being attacked by wolves or bears were pretty foolish, he told himself. Luke's people had been living here for centuries. Also, other kids in these parts rode and walked and went back and forth to school every day.

Naturally they had to be careful. Elie had stressed that above everything. If anything happened to him, she'd probably blame his carelessness. Then he knew at once that she wouldn't. She'd cry. Not with her on-and-off kind of tears either, but the quiet kind he'd seen her crying only once. It was shortly after her mother had quarreled with her father about the Indians. Elie had been huddled in the storeroom with her hands over her face and Booblick licking them. She'd pushed Booblick away when she heard the door close behind Johnny, but otherwise she hadn't tried to bluff it through or smile or anything. She just stood up and walked away.

He'd concluded she was troubled over some of her father's unfair dealings. Then he decided he was probably wrong. A light-hearted girl like her, he felt sure, wouldn't be worrying over Indians. Yet why not, when her mother did. Anyway, in most ways, Boris was an all right father and Elie was lucky to have one.

It was no use thinking of the family or of supper and Mrs. Kirov's good warm bread. He tried to keep his thoughts on Luke and the telescope or even San Francisco but it was no use. His mind always wandered back to the store.

As he emerged from the trees into the open, the terrible bigness of Alaska gripped him again. To the north and east were the great saw-toothed mountains. In front of him lay scrubby hills spreading to far watery flats and all above was a too-big sky. Too big, too high, too pale, and suddenly too empty, even of birds. The few birds he could see were little and skittering, low-down, close to earth as if they were getting ready for night.

His heart pounded with sudden fear, and he started to run. He lost the trail for a while but kept in sight of the river until he found it again. He slowed, gasping and exhausted, then sure the light was going, ran again and stumbled. He tried to catch himself but swung sideways and fell, the telescope banging between him and the rocks. He grabbed the case and even though his knee was bleeding was up instantly.

He had to find shelter, quick, before dusk turned to darkness. Fifty feet away two dwarfed and twisted spruce trees sprawled, growing together out of stone. Johnny limped over to them, looked around and then crawled under the tough, flat spread of their branches. Nursing his knee, and the telescope, he wriggled close to the trunks where a wide break in the stone made a hiding place, then curled himself up there.

Johnny couldn't believe he had slept, yet sunlight was shooting at him down through the tree. He rubbed his eyes. Groaning, he pulled away from the tightness of his nest, sat up on the rock, and looked around. The landscape was every bit as big and wild as he'd thought it was, and he'd spent the night in it. What's more, he didn't feel bad. He had a nasty cut on his knee and a hole in his overalls, but he *hadn't* broken his neck. Or, he hoped, the telescope. He slid down, took it from its case, and turned it carefully in his hands. Adjusting it, he held it to his eye.

The far rocks sprang near and two parka squirrels, playing along the ground, looked close enough to touch. He sat down with a great sigh of relief then raising it again to his eye, watched the squirrels dive in and out of their holes.

Elie had told him they were called parka squirrels because fine warm parkas were often made from their skins. He hoped these two wouldn't end up that way. Suddenly as a shadow flashed near them the squirrels squeaked and were gone. A fox quivered with impatience where they had been.

"Missed them!" breathed Johnny.

The fox, tongue out and eyes bright as glass, retreated a few yards. He sat on his haunches, his fur bristling with attention. His body strained forward as a squirrel popped from its hole and back again, out and back. Then two squirrels tore out, chasing and playing with each other. As the fox tensed to spring, Johnny leapt to his feet and clapped his hands. "Go way!" he yelled.

The squirrels dove back into hiding, the fox loped away in the distance, and Johnny put the telescope back in its case. He might not be able to do much about his own affairs, but he had changed things for a few animals.

Two of them had their busy little lives because of him, and one had an empty stomach.

As empty as mine, he thought, and he felt a sudden friendly feeling for the fox. "Sorry, fella. You'll have to find your breakfast when I'm not looking," he said.

He hit out at a swarm of gnats and settled into a plodding limp along the trail.

Great Salmon Day

11

Johnny thought he could smell the saltiness of the sea long before he saw it lying out there beyond the hills like a great shining, silver platter. He rounded a bluff, and as he came out into the open there was Luke's village almost below him.

Thousands of screaming sea gulls swirled in clouds overhead and the clamor of barking dogs and excited voices came to him clearly. Johnny slipped the telescope from its case and held it to his eye.

A piece of village leaped at him. Then as he moved

the telescope, he caught a confusion of beating, gray-white wings. He lowered it and saw the river, its banks swarming with people – laughing, excited faces, thrashing arms, and flashes of quick-twisting silver. Fish!

Out of the mass, someone slender and quick was running toward him. Luke had seen him coming. "John-ee," he shouted. "Salmon is here."

He hasn't seen the telescope and he's still glad to see *me*, Johnny thought.

Luke's eyes searched Johnny's face with concern. "You come? You all right?" Johnny held out the telescope. "John-ee, what you do?"

Johnny pushed it at him. "It's yours," and as Luke continued to look solemn, Johnny grinned. "Don't worry. I didn't steal it."

Luke broke into smiles. "I know that. You my friend. You speak to Mr. Kirov. You come long way to bring happiness and get fur for taking back."

For a moment, Luke was completely engrossed with the telescope, turning it on the mountains, the village, the shimmer of far water. Training it on the river, he grinned broadly and returned it to its case. "You come on great day, John-ee. Great salmon day. You will stay, see. All right?"

Johnny nodded. He'd tell Luke about his trouble later. Together they went, swinging down to the village where men, women, and children speared and flailed at a leaping tide of salmon surging inward from the sea.

Luke ran to put his telescope safely away and returned to hand Johnny a long-handled scoop, like those he and the others were using. Announcing that Johnny was here as his friend, he found footing for both of them at the edge of the water and they went to work.

With the salmon crowded so close together, catching them wasn't much of a trick. Poor things, thought Johnny, so set on getting where they were supposed to go, to do what they were supposed to do, that worn out or not, battered or not, dying or not, they struggled on. The ones that didn't make it grew into blue-black and silver-bellied piles that slipped and merged with other piles until the river bank was lined with them.

Feet wet, pants wet, sleeves dripping, Johnny became one with the others. Caught with them in an excitement he could plainly feel, he cheered and laughed with them over the tangling of scoops. Over the man who got slapped in the face by a carelessly thrown fish. Over the one who fell in the river and came out clutching the biggest catch of all in his arms. At the fighting of dogs and sea gulls over their share of the feast.

Luke pushed at Johnny, singing a song about salmon people in teasing defiance of the talk they'd once had. Johnny sang back at him the only song he could remember at the moment, "Columbia, Gem of the Ocean."

He thought of Elie and how her eyes would shine at all this. I'll bring her with me next time, he decided, then reminded himself there would probably be no next time. But right now, Johnny Clemens and his cares seemed strangely distant to him. As though some part of him, tired of being sad and worried and discouraged, had decided to be an Indian boy for a while.

He was an Indian, catching food for the winter and singing with his friends. He seemed to feel in himself the flying of the gulls and the leanness of the dogs. He could thank a salmon person for leaving godly flesh and comforts behind to bring food in abundance to his people.

Later he was an Indian boy stuffing himself at the feast, helping the others to bury salmon heads and leftovers in the sand. There they would turn into a sticky-jelly food, a great favorite, *sand salmon*, Luke called it, to be enjoyed much, much later.

In his joy at being accepted, not only by Luke but by all of them, he let himself be talked into wearing a wolf mask and joining in some of the dancing. The painted wooden mask was cleverly carved with a long snout and big teeth, and he felt completely hidden by it.

"What am I supposed to do?" he whispered to Luke.

"Feel like wolf. Move like wolf. *Be* wolf."

Johnny tried. He moved to the beat of rattles and

drums. He did what the others were doing, bending and stamping and swaying, beat, stamp, beat. He tried to *think* wolf, to feel himself stalking a rabbit, a deer. He was a hungry wolf, pacing outside a miner's cabin. He howled, grinning, behind his mask. He went right on telling himself "I am wolf" until the dance was over.

Luke was to do his raven dance alone. He wore black feathers at his shoulders and wrists and a raven mask with a huge hinged beak that was painted red inside. As he danced, he jerked at a sinew cord, making the beak open and close. He seemed to be dancing to say something, to live something, to speak to the raven. He *was* the raven. His feathers shuddered and fluttered the length of his wings as he quivered and circled and dipped. In spite of his hopping, beating feet, his spirit seemed to rise, soaring far above them all into the great upper reaches of sky.

For a while Johnny felt that he was with Luke, almost keeping up, then he slumped, suddenly exhausted. Everything was dark-purpling now. The water held more light than the sky, glowing as though lighted from below. Maybe a few salmon people had stayed at home and were having a party, Johnny thought. Then he shook his head.

It was no use trying to think like Luke any more. It was late and he was tired. He could never in a million years feel another living thing as Luke was feeling the raven. Not that he wouldn't be proud to if he could, proud to be an Indian too if he'd been born one, or brought up like one.

No, he wasn't any good as an Indian. And not doing very well as a white boy either. He was still stuck in Alaska with not even the Kirovs liking him much any more. Could it have been only yesterday that he'd stood watching that schooner and dreaming of leaving? Was it only yesterday he'd talked to that sailor, Bud Riley, who was thinking of jumping ship?

Jumping ship. Johnny shut his mind to the dancing and the drums. If one sailor left ship they would surely need another. And the ship was going to be there, Bud said, for three or four days. If that was true, what could stop him, *really* stop him, from hurrying back tomorrow and trying to get aboard? He was a lot smarter now than he had been a few months ago. A captain would find him harder to get rid of this time.

Could going away be as simple as that? He could scarcely believe it. Of course Boris could stop him if he wanted to. But since Johnny hadn't taken anything but the telescope, he probably wouldn't. There was also that long and dreaded hike back to town. There would be no chance of Luke going with him, not while the salmon were running.

Luke's dance was over, and as he came toward Johnny his eyes had a bright faraway look. He was smiling too, as though at some secret adventure.

"You're the best dancer of all," Johnny told him.

"Because you come and salmon come, I feel much thanks."

Luke spoke so quietly and happily that Johnny decided not to spoil things by telling him about Boris. Let Luke think that he'd sent the telescope, that he was an all-right guy, which, in so many ways, he was.

Johnny had longed for sleep, yet finally lying beside Luke on the sleeping shelf, the telescope between them, he was wide awake. He couldn't wait for morning to come. Outside there were the sounds of talk and laughter as some men of the village, Luke's father among them, continued to catch salmon on through the night. Johnny only half-heard them. He was imagining himself sailing away, half a hundred yards of canvas beating and blowing in the masts over his head.

But before that could happen, he'd have to go to the Kirov's and that would be the hardest part. He'd go by there to pick up his stuff and if they didn't want to talk to him, he'd write a note and leave it on his bed "Thanks for everything. Love, Johnny." The thought came to him that he surely hadn't been much of a prize for them to have around, always moping and criticizing. He might not like Alaska, but they did. Besides, it was their home.

When Johnny woke early the next morning, Luke's father was asleep nearby, but Luke had already gone out. Johnny quickly ate some fish that Luke's mother had prepared and went to the river to find his friend and tell him good-by.

"You must go now? This day?"

Johnny nodded.

"When salmon go, you come back. We go to cliffs. Find white sheep in telescope."

Johnny thought of white sheep and white sails, of wanting to stay and wanting to go. Confused, he turned and did not say good-by.

"Wait," Luke said. "Wolverine skin! I forget." He ran and got it, handing it, carefully rolled, to Johnny. "That one for Mr. Kirov," he said. Then bringing up his other hand, "This for you."

A knife lay across Luke's open palm. Fascinated, Johnny took it. It had a sheephorn pommel carved into a whale's head with two shining shell eyes fitted into the carving. It had a long iron blade and a grip lined with leather. "But why, Luke? Why should you give this to me?"

"You are friend. You come to me without gun, without knife, without knowing of animal ways. For reason that I cannot go with you this day."

"I got here all right, didn't I?"

Luke grinned and nodded. "You know how to use?" He fitted Johnny's hand over the knife grip and thrust it swiftly at the air. "You can do it? All right?"

"I think so." Johnny could hardly speak as he fitted the knife into his belt. He grabbed Luke's hand and shook it. "All right? Sure. Everything's all right and thanks, Luke. Thanks for everything." He turned and started at a half-run, up the hill.

At a place from which he could see the village, he stopped and looked back. The people were waving to him almost as if he were one of them. Pleased, Johnny waved both arms in reply. At the top of the slope he waved again and went on fast.

Both times he'd left this village, he'd been rushing to a ship and this time he had to make it. He *had* to. One hand gripped firmly on the knife head, he let himself think of Aunt May and how changed he would look to her. It shouldn't take her long to see he was not a child any more.

It was a nice day for Alaska. The sky was silver where the sun broke wide under a cloud, white-headed cotton grass grew all along the path, and for once, you could take a deep breath without getting a mouthful of mosquitoes. Elie had said the mosquitoes would leave when the dragonflies came. He decided to look for dragonflies and when he found them, he was as excited as though he'd found the right piece of a puzzle.

He went down on his knees to look closer at a great cluster of them, hovering over grassy flowering moss at the edge of the marsh. Their bodies were a bead-bright blue and green between the shimmer of their wings.

Other colors, pinks and whites and reds and yellows, came from the masses of tiny flowers – perfect little things, beautiful enough to be in a big-city flower shop. And here they were, living and dying in the grass on the edge of nowhere with hardly anyone to notice.

Pretty nice, huh, Pa? The question slipped out easily as though his father were there. Funny the way he was feeling and acting today, as though he might have gotten a dose of Indian magic or something.

Smiling at the thought, he suddenly noticed the sea gulls, whirling hundreds of them. They were screaming and diving over the stream directly down the hill from him. Something else was there too. Unbelieving, he thought he saw a monster of a brown bear standing taller than any man he had ever seen. And then, he knew he had.

Terror shook him. He was afraid to run and afraid not

to. Fearing that any movement might attract the great beast's attention, he stood stock-still. He let out his breath in a slow sigh as the bear dropped to all fours and moved toward the water — toward the water and more bears! Bears and sea gulls and flashing water and salmon. The salmon, escaping upstream from fishing Indians, were now being caught by fishing bears.

Relaxing a little, Johnny watched them. Did the bears, he wondered, count on this time of plenty every year as the Indians did? Did the first ones, spotting salmon, let the others know? Was this their happy time too?

Two bears were fishing from a rocky spit in the middle of the stream with a ring of sea gulls perched, ready for a feed, around them. A mother on the opposite bank slapped at one of her twin cubs when it tried to follow her. Another bear sat up straight in the water, eating as carefully as a human at the fish between its paws.

The monster bear had slipped on a rock, shaken the water from his fur, and was waiting. Johnny felt that he was waiting too and was strangely satisfied when he saw the great paw fasten over leaping silver. The bear, torn fish in its mouth, walked out of the river toward him. It came quickly, but before Johnny could move, it stopped, dropped the fish on a bed of blazing red flowers, pinned it with its paw, and ate.

Johnny ran, stumbled, caught himself, and, afraid to

look back, tore on, far out of sight of the river. It was only when he had to stop at last, to rest, that he started to tremble. Scared stiff, he taunted himself, now that no bear was in sight. Scared, but excited. He felt, as he had yesterday morning, that he might not always feel as lost in the bigness of Alaska as he once had. Back there, for a minute, he'd known that everything belonged, flowers and fish and sea gulls and water. Even the bears. Even himself.

Mountains and sky belonged — it was like a game now, naming things as he rushed, keeping step to his thoughts — dragonflies and mosquitoes, marshes and land, my father and Luke. Kiska and Elie, San Francisco and here. If Elie could hear what I'm thinking, she'd turn it right into a song. Just wait till I tell her about the bears.

The thought sobered him. The quicker he got out of the habit of thinking about the Kirovs, the better. Wait till I tell them in San Francisco, he thought instead.

Hurry Home

12

HE KEPT HIS HAND curved over the hilt of his knife as he walked. The strange brightness of the morning was gone. Thunderheads and darkness were swelling up over the mountains.

Johnny thought of Kiska and wished he were here, running ahead on the leash as he had that day, the wind whipping them both. Funny, he felt different about dogs now. About a lot of things, he guessed. If Kiska had been friendly, it would be great to take him to San Francisco.

His wolfskin, his knife, and a dog, all souvenirs, he'd tell Aunt May, from Alaska. He smiled at the thought. Aunt May, sweet as anything on kids, would take care of the dog in a hurry.

"Ugh! His great muddy paws!" He could almost hear her say it. "Johnny, *honey*! Houses are not for animals. Out, you. Out!"

Johnny shivered and waited for the thunder as lightning sliced crookedly through a great black cloud above him. It came. Then, almost beside him, a whistle sounded from the rocks. Johnny jumped, furious with himself for being scared by a furry little pika, no bigger than a squirrel. Immediately, there was another sound, a great clattering gallop, as a horse with someone astride bore down upon him. The rider waved and pulled the horse up short so that dust and pebbles flew from its hooves. It was Bud Riley, the young sailor he'd talked to two days before.

"Hello, there," Bud said. "This the right trail?"

"To where?"

"To see the Indians. Say, aren't you one of the welcoming committee that met me when I landed?"

"Yes, I am. You going to quit the ship?"

"Expected to find you at the Indian village. At least I guess you're the one. Your family at the Bee Kay said if I saw you to give you a message. Two words. 'Hurry home.' The salmon running?"

Johnny nodded. Family? he wondered.

"Hey, did you hear me?"

"Salmon? Oh, yeah millions of them."

"Heard they were bound upstream and that it's a sight to see. Say, that's quite a knife you're wearing. You guarding whatever you got inside your coat?"

"No. It's a fur. Got it in trade for the Bee Kay. Wolverine." Johnny showed it to him. "If you're leaving the ship, I. . . ."

"Never saw a skin like that before. How much?" Bud interrupted.

"You'll have to ask Boris Kirov. You jumping ship? Because if you are, I want your job."

"You leaving your family or something?"

Johnny glared at him. Where'd he get that *family* stuff?

Bud grinned. "Something you don't like about this place? I was figuring I might settle here."

"I thought you were going on to the Klondike."

"I like it here. Wonderful country. Opportunities, too. They tell me a lumber mill's going up. And a cannery."

The horse skittered at a cloud of gnats and Johnny jumped back. "I need to know if you're going to stay," he shouted, "so I can ask for your job on the ship."

"You want to, you can likely get on regardless of what I do. I'm going back with them this time but two of our hands beat it for the Chilkoot yesterday."

"Oh," Johnny said.

"And if the *Davy M.* won't take you, the *Fortuna* will. Big old tub of a ship, just got in this morning. They tried to sign up some of our men. Seems a couple of theirs jumped overboard farther down the coast and swam for it. Maybe they'd been shanghaied in the first place. Who knows? The way I heard it, they're also losing a few to the goldfields. Lucky if they have enough left to make a crew. You want to ship out there's nothing to stop you."

Now that what he had waited so long and hard for was apparently easy, Johnny could think of nothing to say.

Bud leaned down to him. "What don't you like about it here? Give me one reason why I shouldn't come back here to stay. Steady there, flyer," he soothed the horse and turned again to Johnny. "One little reason."

Johnny shrugged. "Your coming back is *your* business," he said. "My *not* staying is mine."

"That's right." Bud grinned. "One thing here, they're pretty lax when it comes to law. I noticed that already. Looks like Uncle Sam forgot Alaska almost as soon as he bought it." He leaned out of the saddle and winked. "Why don't we stick around and clean up the place?"

"You can. I'm going home."

"Home?"

"To San Francisco."

"Why didn't you say so? I thought. . . ." Bud rolled his eyes. "I guess I thought. . . ."

"And be careful of bears." Johnny grinned. "They're fishing the river three or four miles from here, but if you keep going they'll probably pay no attention to you."

"Bears! You joshing?"

"That's another thing about Alaska," Johnny shouted above the wind, the words coming easy now, "bears and mosquitoes and mud and rain and freezing and. . . ."

"How'd you keep coming if there were bears?"

"They were busy. Fishing."

"You serious?"

"Sure. Getting their share of the salmon run. Six or seven of them when I came by."

"I'm not tangling with any bears. Besides the sky's going to open any minute. Climb on, I'll take you back," he said and boosted Johnny up behind him. "Old man I met told me I was daft to bother seeing Indians. 'There's nothin' out there to see,' he said, 'nothin' at all.' "

"The old man's the daffy one," Johnny said, as they bounced along. "The Indian village is only the most interesting place I've ever seen, that's all. The people are different too."

"What do you mean, different?"

"Oh, I don't know." He tried to think. "Calm, except for salmon time. Steady. You know, dignified. My friend out there told me his tribe's been crossing the Chilkoot to trade with inland tribes since early times."

"You got a friend out there?" Bud looked surprised.

"Yes. Luke. The best friend I've ever had," and for the first time he was telling someone about his father's death.

When he'd finished, Bud turned and stuck out his hand. "You have had a time," he said. "Glad to know you. You've got spunk."

Johnny shook hands, embarrassed. "If I can't get on your ship I'll have to take my chances on that other one. Nothing or anyone is going to keep me here any longer."

"Here it comes!" Bud cried as the rain broke over them.

It blew hard in their faces, hammered at rocks and leaves, pock-marked, then muddied the dust of the trail. It darkened the dusty clothes of plodding miners, and dripped from the rims of their hats. The horse lowered its head into it, gave an impatient snort and trotted on.

"Turn here," Johnny said when they reached the main street. "I'll show you the only part of town that I like."

From horseback, the flowers in the frontyard of Mrs. Monahan's place, looked like a bright wet quilt.

"Biggest blooms I ever saw," Bud said. "Hey, rain's stopping already."

"Yeh."

Mrs. Monahan, standing on her front porch, waved as they went by. So did Mr. Appleton, halfway through sawing a log. "Where you think you're going, Johnny?" he called out.

Mr. Jack, sitting under a black umbrella in the doorway of his feed and grain store, shouted to him, laughingly, that he was going to get wet.

"Seems like everyone knows you," Bud said.

"I guess a few do." Realizing it for the first time gave Johnny a strange feeling.

"Look," Bud said, "I think I'll drop you off now that the rain has let up. I hired this horse for all day. Might as well keep him all day. Think I'll go back along that gold trail. Give some old gold digger a lift and find out what he's got to say for himself."

"How do I get to the ship to make sure they'll take me?"

"Stick around the pier. A few hands will be making trips back and forth today, working. I got out of that deal. Did my stint at Ketchikan. You don't have to worry about them taking you, but you ought to make arrangements. Captain's a stickler for that. Runs a good show. See you later," he said, as Johnny slipped down.

Johnny waved to him and stood for a moment, trying to get the self-confidence to walk freely, head up, along the street. He passed the Nugget Bar, Joe's Tin and Hardware, Poultice and Pills, the Cloverleaf Bar, Mrs. Morgan's Food House, and the Bee Kay. Kiska was on the porch. He lifted his head, ears up. They stared at each other for a moment before Johnny hurried on.

He pushed through the noisy, crowded street and was running toward the pier, when he sensed *something* behind him. He turned. Kiska was following him.

"Go!" he shouted and ran faster, not looking back again until he reached the pier. Kiska stood at a distance, watching him.

A rowboat holding one sailor and a huge barrel was pulled up by the pier. Another sailor was ready to push it off.

"You going out to the *Davy M.*?"

"Plan to."

"Will you take me, please?"

"What for?"

"To ask the captain for a job."

"Pretty big for your breeches, ain't you? Got a wicked knife there too, I see. Might be you're planning to use it."

"Oh, let the kid alone." The other sailor beckoned, and Johnny splashed through the water and into the boat.

"Sit down! You want to dunk us! Get in the stern there. Careful. Put your back to the water barrel, keep her from rolling."

Johnny crouched down, the barrel bruisingly heavy against his back. Off to his left, he could see the steamer *Fortuna,* shabby and uninteresting compared to the trim, masted cleanness of the *Davy M.* Before him, the town looked like a picture: mountains, houses, shore, and sea, all shining under a sunburst sky. It was so pretty it made him ache inside. Or perhaps the ache was excitement about what he was going to do.

The captain was lean, white-haired, and stern looking. "I've been expecting you," he said when they climbed aboard.

"Me?" Johnny's voice broke in a foolish squeak.

The captain smiled. "A fellow was here a while ago with a load of mail to go out, asking for you. At least I presume it was you. Your name Johnny Clemens?"

"Yes, sir."

"He said if you hadn't stayed with some Indian friends you might try to come aboard. He asked me if I was sure you weren't here already and I asked him, 'You speaking of a stowaway?' "

Johnny burned with sudden anger. So Boris *was* trying to stop him. "Ask the sailors who brought me whether I was trying to hide," he shouted at the captain. "I came to ask for a job, any job to get home."

"Just what Kirov said you'd say." The captain looked amused. "His interest in the matter, he told me, was to make sure, job or not, we'd be willing to take you."

"Oh," Johnny said. His legs felt like rubber as the relief he was waiting for didn't come. Only the old remembering that he was alone came, with its heavy sadness. "Then you *will* let me work," he said.

"I could surely use some help. Lost two men with gold fever. You'd have to keep busy. No fooling around."

"I know."

"We've got a hold full of rock salt waiting for the load of salmon we're going to pick up down the coast. However, I understand from Kirov that he'd be glad to pay for your passage. In which case, of course, you wouldn't have to work. Think it over. Let me know which way you want it."

"I'll work."

"You can start now if you want. That your gear under your jacket? That all you got?"

"No. My gear's at the Kirov's."

"Couple of the crew are going ashore for more water shortly. They'll take you. If you're coming aboard in the morning, come early. We sail at eleven."

"All right, sir. Thank you."

Kiska was waiting at the end of the pier. Together, yet not together – the dog never really walking with him – they made their way to the store.

It was perfectly clear to Johnny now that Boris was through with him. Probably all the Kirovs were. The message they'd sent to him by Bud to hurry home was clear now, too. They weren't taking any chances on his missing that boat. He had to force himself, lifting his legs slowly, one by one, to climb the trading-post steps and go in.

Mrs. Kirov was waiting on the fat, blonde waitress from across the street. "Hello, Johnny," she said. Smiling, she handed him an oil can to be filled.

He dropped the rolled skin on the counter and took the can. In the storeroom he listened as the businesslike sound of coal oil gurgled from the big can filling the little one. He remembered how he used to hate the smell of it and that he didn't any more. He remembered that once, when he had been tidying up this big, dark, shelf-lined room, the thought had come to him that Boris liked him.

No Longer Guns

13

"BORIS AND ELIE are out somewhere," Mrs. Kirov said.

She was looking at him, straight and steady. There was something in her look though, something he couldn't understand, that made him feel more ill at ease than ever. "You didn't see them?"

Johnny shook his head, waiting awkwardly as the few words he'd planned to say in parting, stuck in his throat.

Mrs. Kirov reached for the wolverine skin, spread it out, and stroked it. "Too many who come here want only to reach the Yukon," she said. "They only want, any way they can, to find gold and then, any way they can, get back to the states with it. Never once thinking Alaska is part of the greatness of America, or caring. If those who *do* have some idea of living here in a civilized way, under law, if they all leave us, what then?"

She didn't look up and Johnny wondered, confused, Is she asking *me*?

"If you mean me," he said at last, "I'm not a man."

"You will be."

"I know," he faltered, "but. . . ."

"Already you have reminded a good man, and Boris *is* a good man, of something very important to him and all of us. Something, I fear, that he was beginning to forget."

"I. . . ." He felt his face flush. "But he. . . ." He stammered and stopped.

"Dear Johnny," she said and laughed. "Forget it! What am I thinking of? Of course you're a boy. What's more, the only reasons, the only longings you must ever listen to *must* be your own. Will you watch the store for me till they come? I've got a stew going upstairs."

Feeling as though he had no right to be there, Johnny walked behind the counter and sat down. Kiska followed, dropping heavily beside him. Johnny bent over determined to pet him but stopped as the door opened and Elie came in.

She took one look and called back over her shoulder, "Papa! Johnny's here."

"Hello, Elie," Johnny said.

"So you came back," she said in her uppity way.

Johnny shrugged. He didn't see how she could seem so pleased to see him, and yet be giving him the cold shoulder at the same time.

"If you think I'm glad you're home so that you can go away to stay," she said, "well, I'm not."

"Maybe I didn't expect you to be. I came to get my things."

"You don't care much for *anyone*, do you?"

"Don't be silly."

"When Papa. . . ."

Boris came in then and told her to go upstairs.

"But I haven't had a chance to talk to him at all."

"Go on," he said, and she called Booblick and went.

Slowly, Johnny stood up.

Boris grinned. "You and Kiska sign a truce?" He asked it in his best be-nice-to-the-customers voice.

Johnny didn't answer, didn't smile. He pointed to the fur.

"It's a nice skin," Boris said, examining it. "A very nice skin. You think you made me a profitable trade?"

Johnny felt himself trembling. "I didn't have anything

to do with it. Luke sent it to you in return for the telescope. *He's* satisfied."

"Fair enough. That sailor, Bud, find you?"

Johnny nodded. "I knew about the ship. I was already on my way back because of it."

"I see," Boris said. "Then you'll be interested to know they've got room and plenty for you aboard should you care to go. I took the mail over this morning and spoke to the captain."

"I know. He told me."

"You've been there? You're going, then?"

"I am, don't worry," Johnny said, and he tried to laugh. "To think I was fretting about our contract. That you mightn't let me break it, I mean."

"Nothing in our contract said you had to work for a cheater. . . ." Boris's voice broke and he turned away.

"You're not. You're really not a cheater, Boris," Johnny cried. "I mean, with me you weren't, ever! With me, you. . . ." Embarrassed and unable to find the right words, Johnny started to walk away. Then he felt Boris's hand, firm and friendly, on his shoulder.

"Maybe we'd better stick to business, Johnny. Fact is, I'd dreamed up a little proposition in that line. But no use going into that, now that your mind's made up."

"My mind's *always* been made up. You know that. That was the whole point of everything. I *have* to go."

"I guess you do." He cupped one of Johnny's hands and dropped some gold coins into it. "Three twenties and three tens. That's what's due you for the time you worked. With some thrown in for good behavior as I promised. Good behavior, I said, and I mean it. You might have used a little more tact in letting me know what you thought of me, but for a young fellow, well, Johnny I want to show you something."

He went to the ledger and flipped the back pages until a yellowed, dog-eared card fell out. Johnny picked it up.

"That's it. That's what I was looking for. Read it."

Printed on the card were six words in big, bold letters.

REMEMBER, BORIS — NO LONGER GUNS. EVER.

Boris smiled at Johnny's puzzlement. "I wrote that the day I decided to go into business. As a reminder to myself."

"I don't know what it means," Johnny said. "No longer guns."

"Well, I'll tell you. I knew an old Eskimo when I was a kid, used to tell me about his dealings with the Yankee trading ships. The traders would measure the height of his pile of spread-out skins with a gun. When the pile was as high as the gun, the Eskimo got the gun and the Yankees got the furs. Each year, he told me, the guns got longer and longer. I grew up hating those Yankee frauds. Pledged I'd never be one, wrote that card to remind me, and thought I'd never forget it." He sighed, put the card back in the book, and closed it. "I won't from here on, but that's neither here nor there. To get back to the subject, you can work your way or sail in style. It's up to you. The money's yours."

"Thank you very much." To hide his feelings, Johnny ducked down beside Kiska. The dog, he'd noticed, had been sitting on its haunches, ears up, eyes attentive, as though it understood every word. Johnny stroked his head easily. "Boris?"

"What?"

"Was paying me the proposition you were thinking about?"

"No, I told you. You earned the pay."

"What, then?"

"No point now. I did have quite a speech to go with it, though. Big new stake in promised land, stuff like that," he chuckled.

Johnny laughed with him. "What else?"

"Staying. Helping me part time in the business in return for a share in it. Go to school, visit your friend, Luke, do what you want the rest of the time. Looked to me like each of us could teach the other something." He rolled the wolverine skin and put it under the counter. "I had it all figured out just fine."

"You mean I'd belong here."

"Sure. If you happened to feel the same, that is, and weren't expected or needed somewhere else. Confound it, it wouldn't have to be something a fellow'd decide for life. As if he couldn't change his mind after one year or two or ten and sell out his share."

He stopped as Johnny dropped one of the coins. "Come here." He reached in a drawer and took out a small buckskin bag with a drawstring, the type used to carry gold dust. He handed it to Johnny. "Never keep all your money in the same purse when you're traveling."

"Thanks. Thanks for everything but I have to go, Boris. It's all I've ever thought about since Pa died."

"I know." Boris nodded. "And, what's more, it's *your* life. You planning to go aboard in the morning?"

"Yes, sir."

"That's that, then. Now, how about it? You hungry?"

"I'm starved!"

He was sure no one had ever paid attention to him as Elie did that evening while they were eating. She seemed to listen with all of herself, eyes, mouth, hands, even her shoulders hunched toward him, as he told about the salmon run, the dancers, and the bears. He had to laugh, the way her face seemed so *hers* all of a sudden, as though an outline he knew very well had become filled in.

The room was like that too, in a way, and Boris's and Mrs. Kirov's faces. So was the view from the window. It made him wonder, coming and going as he'd been most of his life, if he hadn't too often seen only the outlines of things. People too — seen them flat, like drawings, only real where their lives touched his.

His thoughts flashed to Aunt May's face and Uncle Bill's. To her letter, "*my poor little Johnny. . . .*"

"Now what are you thinking about?" Elie asked.

"My aunt and uncle. Do you think they'll believe what I've been telling you?"

"You know something, Johnny? You haven't been here four months yet and already you talk more like a *sourdough* than a *cheechako*. That proves you ought to. . . ."

"Careful, Elie," her mother said.

"They're so afraid I'll make you feel bad, begging you to stay. As if that isn't the most important thing to me. As if. . . ."

"Elie!"

Her mother's reproving voice and Boris's, calling to him, came at the same moment.

"Friend to see you, Johnny."

"It couldn't be Luke. Or could it?" he said to Elie as he ran downstairs.

It was Bud. "You going?" he asked.

"Sure," Johnny answered.

"Now?"

"No. In the morning. I haven't even got my stuff together yet."

"Come on anyway. Walk as far as the pier with me."

"I'm sort of tired."

"Oh, come on."

Johnny didn't know why, but he didn't particularly care to go right then. It was as though he'd been doing something he wasn't ready to have interrupted. Yet he could think of no good excuse for not going.

He looked at Boris. "Anything I can do here to help you?"

Boris waved him off. "We'd better get used to doing without you, don't you think?" And, as Kiska started after them, "Kisk! Stay! They don't want to be bothered with you. Stay! I said."

Johnny looked back as he and Bud reached the street and saw Elie standing in the upstairs window. He waved, but she didn't wave back. Looking again, he saw Kiska lurking behind them.

"Go back, Kiska," he said.

"I thought at first those people were your family," Bud said. "They kind of act like it. Even the dog acts like it."

"You think so? Seems to me he's more watching than liking me."

"You don't know much about dogs, do you? Hello, Kiska."

"All I know is that the first time he saw me, I thought

he was going to tear me apart." To reassure himself that it was no longer true, Johnny held out his hand and when Kiska came to him, he stroked his ears. "Kisk, Boris said to stay with *him*. You'd better go back now. Go!" he ordered, pointing until the dog started slowly back, stopping at intervals to watch them.

Johnny's Compass

14

THEY SAT, hugging their knees and watching the sunset, in the bottom of a *Davy M*. rowboat. It was pulled up on the shore in the shadow of the pier, where Bud had left it that morning.

"Just look, will you!" Bud exclaimed. "A couple of hours before midnight and look at it! I don't care how you feel about this country. I love it."

Johnny didn't answer. It was pretty. The way colors glowed on the dark water reminded him of the opals in a brooch his mother used to wear. It was strange the way people and things and what you've done in your life stayed alive. You thought they were gone and then, click, there they were, as real as anything else.

"Is the *Fortuna* going to San Francisco, too?" he asked Bud.

"I guess so. Johnny, I've been dreamin' about something. The *Davy M.*'s bound for China after Frisco. How about signing up with me for the long trip?"

"I thought you were coming back here," Johnny teased him. "I thought you liked this country so much."

"I am. I do. Later. Plenty of time for settling down. Think of it. China! How about it?"

"Fine." Johnny laughed. "If you want to go there. I don't."

"Why not? Where *do* you want to go then?"

A clear picture suddenly came to him of Luke trailing a white sheep on a wild hillside. "San Francisco," he said impatiently. "I told you before."

"All right, all right. I only asked. Look, a boat's coming in from the *Fortuna*."

They watched it come toward them, bow and oars breaking the colored water. "Wonder when they're sailing," Bud said; and, as two men jumped out and pulled the boat on shore, he asked them, "Your ship going soon?"

"Soon enough."

"Bound for Frisco?"

"Where else?" The words were hardly more than a grunt as the larger of the two men pushed his cap back from his shaggy hair and looked them over.

"You interested?" The smaller man came close to them, wheedling. "We'll make you a proposition. Best life in the world for a kid, a sailor's life. Good food. Good pay. Sea nymphs, dolphins, Africa, Araby. . . ."

"We're already shipping out," Bud said. "On the *Davy M.*"

As the big man strode away, the small one spat and spoke fast. "You don't have to, do you? They don't own you, do they? You show promise, you get a share of cargo profits with us."

When Bud looked at him hard and grinned without speaking, he put his hands in his pockets and went.

Bud whistled. "A genteel pair, what?" After a moment, he began to speak of himself. He was the oldest child of five, he said, and had been making his own way for several years, mostly at sea.

"I was brought up in the big California valley and without ever seeing the ocean, I knew it was for me. I've worked on half a dozen ships, but give me a schooner any time. Those sails speak to me when they're spread and filling. You know what I mean?"

"I think so."

"Well, guess I'd better be getting back before they think I've jumped."

"Tell the captain I'll be early." Johnny helped him push the boat into the water and watched Bud row out to the schooner.

China, he thought, and leaned against the pier, puzzling. Some people, like Luke and Elie, seemed to have built-in compasses to point their way. Others, like his father and Bud, did fine without any. For a while, anyway. What wouldn't he give to have one!

He remembered the good feeling he'd sometimes gotten as he marked off the days on his calendar. Now, with the ship right out there ready to leave with him on it, why couldn't he feel that way again? Had too much happened to him in the last few days or was he just too tired to feel anything?

He waved, in case Bud might still be able to see him, and started back to the noise and the lights. This time tomorrow, he thought, trying to cheer himself, I'll be a long, long way from here.

"Hey, boy." The voice came from a narrow alley between the buildings. Johnny peered into the shadows and recognized the little man from the *Fortuna.* Before he could decide whether to answer or run, a great hand was slapped over his mouth and his hands were pinned behind him.

"Tell him!" the big man ordered, and the small one spoke close to Johnny's face.

"Listen, kid. Don't panic. We're going to Frisco and you're going to Frisco. That's where you want to go, ain't it?"

"Ain't it?" he insisted as Johnny struggled and strained to get loose, to shake his head, to call for help.

When only a stifled squeak came from him, the big man laughed. He tightened his hand on Johnny's mouth and pinned his body closer to his own. "With all that racket goin' on next door, you think anybody's goin' to hear you? Go on," he snarled at the little man, "tie his hands."

As Johnny tried to wrench his wrists apart, they jerked them together with a dirty rag, tightened, and tied it. "We gotta have a crew to run a ship," the little sailor complained. "And don't think we wouldn't rather have a man-sized one. Might yet before the night's out. But a kid's better than nothin' if he'll work, and you will. You better!"

"Stop that gaff and give me the other rag. Ouch!" Johnny had ground his teeth into the hand at his mouth. He forced a weak cry before a wad of cloth was forced into his mouth and almost down his throat.

"Now, try to make a sound, curse you!"

Johnny gagged, trying desperately to spit out the wad.

Then he saw Kiska.

The dog rushed the men and was on them in one great snarling leap before they knew what was happening. The little man fell backward; the big one gave Johnny a savage shove and went for Kiska. Johnny struck the wall behind him as he fell. Half-stunned, he struggled to his feet, as men and dog tangled in a growling, cursing melee. Johnny worked frantically to free his hands. When he saw a knife flash, he ran.

Staggering and dizzy, he tripped off the boardwalk, fell to his knees, and retched. He retched till the gag came out, then, sobbing with rage, forced the bands loose from his hands and started back toward the alley.

A man, coming out a saloon door, called to him, "What's the matter, boy?"

"Them!" Johnny pointed. "Kisk! Kiska!" he yelled.

He let out a whoop of relief as Kiska came bounding out of the shadows. "Good Kisk!"

Together they tore along the streets to the Bee Kay. Johnny flung open the door. "Boris!" Boris rushed forward from the back of the store. "Oh Boris," Johnny cried, "They tried to make me go!"

With Boris's arm around his shaking shoulders, Johnny blurted out what had happened. "If they'd hurt Kiska. . . !" he finished.

"Let's have a look at him."

Together they bent down beside the panting dog. They found a badly bruised groin and a knife slit in his ear. "That ear will heal in a hurry," Boris said. "Don't worry about that. He'll be fine. Turn in now, Johnny, and get some rest. I'm going out. I want to speak to some fellows about that *Fortuna* pair. See you before you leave in the morning. All right?"

Johnny had been lying on his bed fully dressed for at least half an hour, and he still couldn't stop trembling. But why? He was safe, wasn't he? Kiska was going to be all right and nothing was changed about his going on the *Davy M*. So, what was he shaking about? Why couldn't he stop? The words *They tried to make me go* kept running through his head.

He ought to be getting his things together. His clothes, a few things of his father's, his wolfskin. The knife from Luke and some special rocks that Elie had given him. He wondered whether she was asleep yet and whether Luke and his family were still catching salmon.

Get going, he ordered himself but he didn't move. He heard Boris come back in the store and bolt the door before he went upstairs. He heard the familiar squeak of floorboards overhead. He heard a sound outside his door and, telling himself it couldn't be, sat up to listen.

It came again. Johnny leaped to the door, and Kiska

bounded in. "Good dog. My dog. Mine." Johnny was down on his knees, hugging him. He looked into the dog's eyes and examined his hurt ear. "Do you like me?" he whispered, and when Kiska's tail waved, Johnny hugged him again.

Suddenly, he ran to the window and pulled down the shades. He lighted the lamp and, imagining winter, set another lighted match to the kindling in the stove. As he waited for it to flare up, he carefully spread the wolfskin like a rug on the floor before it, sat down on it, and invited Kiska to join him. Kiska cocked his head to one side and, as Johnny patted the wolfskin again, dropped heavy and warm beside him. Johnny gently moved the big head to rest on his knee. "My dog," he said and they sat quietly together.

"Johnny?" It was Elie's voice at the door.

"Come in."

"Papa told me I could say good night," she said solemnly, as she stepped into the room. "What are you doing?"

Johnny shrugged and laughed and, hearing himself, laughed again. It was as though something inside him was pointing straight and perfectly true.

"I guess I don't want to go anywhere." He laughed as he said it. "Not anywhere at all."

"Johnny! You mean . . .?"

He nodded and she ran to the door. "Mama! Papa! Come quick! The most wonderful thing has happened!"